I0764295

Best Gay Stories 2011

Best Gay Stories 2011

edited by Peter Dubé

~ ~ ~

Lethe Press
Maple Shade NJ

www.lethepressbooks.com lethepress@aol.com

Book Design by Toby Johnson
Published by Lethe Press, 118 Heritage Avenue, Maple Shade, NJ 08052.

Trade paperback:
ISBN-13: 978-1-59021-227-1
ISBN-10: 1-59021-227-4

Case laminate library binding:
ISBN-13: 978-1-59021-226-4
ISBN-10: 1-59021-226-6

INTRODUCTION

Welcome to *Best Gay Stories 2011*, the first edition of this fine series not to be edited by the formidable Steve Berman.

It's a strange thing to take over the editing of an already established anthology series, one with a well-defined mandate. Certainly Steve's sensible shoes will not be easy for me to fill. That's why I hesitated when he asked if I'd be interested in the job; to be honest, it took me a couple of months to get back to him while I mulled over a few things. Things like the fact that an anthology of this sort is one over which readers enjoy arguing; everyone has an idea of his or her own what a particular year's best stories might have been, and they are unlikely to agree with every choice an editor makes. Even as one is working to put the book together one anticipates the comments about to be made by any number of reviewers. So, lets be upfront about it; the stories contained in this anthology may or may not appear on any other individual's list of bests, but they are all very fine stories, and they're among the ones I, as an editor, liked the best this year. I liked them for diverse reasons. And, as you'll see, "diversity" is an important word in connection with this volume.

I highlight "diversity" because all too often the representations of gay men's lives to be found in the general media suggest that gay life and culture is some towering, right-angled, monolithic structure; that we all go to the same bars, shop in the same stores, eat in the same restaurants, hold the same kinds of political opinions, have similar backgrounds, and work the same kinds of jobs (more often than not urban and vaguely white-collar.) The clichés of the gay ghetto and its pink dollar still hold sway out there, it seems. In movies and television shows the sort-of hip and unwaveringly supportive gay best friend is a constant. (Who has these crazy one-sided friendships, anyway?) In the newspapers we're angry activists or predatory threats to traditional families. On talk radio...well don't ask. Anyway, if you're reading this, chances are you know.

But when we get to step up to the proverbial microphone and tell our own stories, well—then—something other than that monolith appears. A different picture is revealed, or rather different *pictures* are revealed. In our writing, to borrow the old saw of gay liberation movements past, we are everywhere. In cities and country, offices and factories and shops and academies. We work and we fuck, we shout and we steal. We love each other and, yes, we hurt each other. When we tell our own stories, it becomes clear that we've moved well past the sentimental coming-out story, the boy-meets-boy romance, the dangers and pleasures of sexual adventure, and we've done it without having to abandon them—because those things still happen and are still important. But we've found new ways of thinking about them, and have *more* experience to share, a deeper understanding of them, and we've added an array of other stories, from other parts of our lives and dreams and troubles to them. We've moved past the "gay story" and towards "gay stories."

This book wants to add to that shift—a process of complicating ideas of gay life, of proliferating images and accounts and possibilities. It's what I hope this book is all about; the way we come to understand our lives by recounting them, by finding a way to explain how one thing affects another, how one thing—a person, a place, a feeling or a perception—connects to the next and how we make sense of all that. I see *Best Gay Stories* as being committed to the power and potential of the act of storytelling, the narrative impulse itself. And in all its different forms.

So, in these pages are a magnificent assortment of narratives and an equally fabulous range of ways of narrating them. The book includes experimental work and traditional tales, fantasy and realism, and as many different perspectives as one might hope to find. It includes work by well-established authors, and by some newer names. It includes work that might traditionally be shelved as "genre" fiction and some other pieces that might be adjudged more "literary" by critics still clinging to such categories. It also includes work by men and women, because I wanted gay stories—not necessarily just gay writers. To be honest, these things were not my primary focus while I was reading. I was looking for a good piece of writing, something that moved me, or challenged me, or gave me pleasure. A story that said something I hadn't heard before, or said it in a way I hadn't heard before. I was reading for stories that went someplace unexpected, or that laid claim to language we might not have used once upon a time. Mostly, I was looking for stories I knew I'd want to read again. And again. I think I found some, indeed a diversity of them. And I hope you think so too.

So—*vive la difference.* And once again, welcome to *Best Gay Stories 2011*.

Peter Dubé

Table of Contents

SANDRA McDONALD

Sandra McDonald's impressive debut collection, *Diana Comet and Other Improbable Stories*, was a Booklist Editor's Choice for 2010, an American Library Association "Over the Rainbow" book, and a winner of the Lambda Literary Award. Her short fiction about transgender ghosts, sexy cowboy robots and more has appeared in more than forty markets, and her science fiction novels follow an Australian military lieutenant and her handsome sergeant. She earned an MFA in Creative Writing at the University of Southern Maine and teaches college in Northeast Florida. Visit her at sandramcdonald.com.

Diana Comet and the Lovesick Cowboy

Sandra McDonald

In about five minutes the lovesick cowboy was going to lurch off his lumpy bed, grab his pistol, stumble out to the balcony of this fleabag hotel and shoot every last bullet down into the saloon across the street. Justifiable homicide, some slick lawyer might say. No man should have to listen to "Campside Traces" a dozen times in a row on a broiling hot summer day. Murdering the piano player would be doing the entire town of Goldstone a favor, and maybe afterward the mayor would pin a hero's medal on Sam Landan's chest.

Landan didn't want medals. He'd had medals, once upon a time. They were scattered now, like silver and gold birds, lost to pawn shops or barroom bets on the journey west. All he really wanted was his Isaac, who was out there in the hills hopefully just as miserable and lonely as he was. But unless that stubborn fool saw reason, Landan would have to make do with alcohol.

That wretched song began again. Maybe it would be more expeditious to shoot himself instead of the pianist.

He wouldn't have to walk so far, and there was less chance of hurting someone innocent. Then again, the walls were so flimsy any bullet through his temple might just arc through the plaster and hit his neighbors—the ladies of ill repute over in room 206, or the recluse with the awful cough over in room 202. To be a true gentleman he'd have to shoot up through his chin. Luckily the ceiling already had so many holes in it that one more wasn't likely to make a difference.

Instead of shooting himself he grabbed the whiskey bottle and drained the last precious gulp. His last swallow coincided with a brisk knock on the door. Surely a mistake. The room was paid up through the week, and nobody in town had business with him. But there was that knock again, brisk and demanding, so Landan staggered over to turn the doorknob.

The woman in the hallway was beautiful and proper in a way that made him think he was hallucinating. Despite the heat, she was impeccably dressed in a royal blue jacket, ankle-length skirt, and fancy leather shoes. Her dark hair was swept up and pinned under a satin hat decorated with lace. She was in her mid thirties or so, not so much older than Landan, but obviously from the world he'd long put aside—the world of cities and boulevards, fancy tea parties and ballrooms filled with fine folk.

"Captain Samuel Landan?" she asked optimistically.

"Not anymore." Legs unsteady, he leaned against the doorframe. "Who are you?"

Undaunted, she said, "My name is Diana Comet. I've come from Massasoit. I want to hire Captain Landan to take me out to the Circle W ranch in Kelly's Pass."

Landan liked the word "hire." More money meant more whiskey. The Circle W, that was no problem. Long haul to get there, but he'd heard good words about the place from the men who worked the pass. Yet despite the positive omens, this fine-looking city woman in her very fine attire seemed like a series of headaches waiting to happen; she'd harangue him about drinking, maybe try to get him to go to church, and heaven help him if she ever found out he was a sinner and a sodomite.

"He's not for hire," he said.

"I hear differently," Miss Comet said. "And I pay very well."

"Sorry." Landan closed the door in her face.

After dark, with the noise of miners and cowboys filling the town and a powerful thirst urging him on, he slapped tepid water on his face and went down to see what money he could win at poker. To his surprise, Miss Comet was waiting for him in a chair across from the front desk. She held a book in her lap. She seemed serenely unconcerned with the drunken men careening about in the company of perfumed and painted women.

"I'll buy you dinner," she said.

He considered. "Buy me whiskey."

"Dinner and one whiskey. Shall we?"

She led him down the street to the town's only reputable hotel, where the dining room had red velvet paper on the walls and a waiter in relatively clean clothes served them chicken with potatoes. He couldn't remember the last time he'd eaten with polished silverware. Miss Comet let him have his one whiskey, and then despite every urge in his body he ordered coffee.

"What do you want with the Circle W?" he asked.

Her expression was somber. "I've come to check on the welfare of an orphan boy sent there a year ago to find a new home."

"The Circle W's closer to Flagpole than here. You could have taken the stagecoach straight through."

"The coach broke an axle on the way from Elizabeth City," she said. "And the next one's not due for two days. I need a local guide to get me to the Circle W."

Landan sipped his bitter coffee. "Are you a missionary?"

"A philanthropist."

"That's a fancy word, ma'am."

"Not too big for Captain Landan. He attended East Point. Graduated near the top of his class. A most promising officer, they said."

Landan hadn't thought about the academy in a long time. He remember the grand granite buildings, the sweeping parade grounds, the view across the North River to the sprawling metropolis of Massasoit. The city was a dream of spires and chimneys soaring upward, and steel bridges flinging outward, and a lingering haze of smoke and steam and the noise of multitudes. The river itself, strong but complacent in summer, churned and teemed with thunderous ice during the winter. The memory of so much water seemed to him surreal and slightly obscene after all the dry land of mining country. Isaac had never been anywhere east of Texana; Landan had tried to describe the North River to him once, as they both lay naked and sated by the edges of a creek, but he'd flatly refused to believe in such a sight.

He reached for more coffee. "You can't believe everything people chatter on about, Miss Comet."

"If it's a matter of money, I assure you that you'll be promptly and accurately paid. If it's pride, rest assured that I've seen men fall into worse conditions after honorable military service during war. If it's an addiction to liquor that keeps you here, then simply say so and I won't bother you any further."

Her gaze was forthright, her voice clear, and for the first time in a long time Landan realized he was in the presence of a woman of candor and ambition. She was also the most beautiful woman he'd seen since the war. Yet there was something in her chin, or maybe the symmetry of her eyes, that nagged at the edges of his frayed nerves. Maybe he'd seen her portrait somewhere, or known a cousin of hers.

His brain itched. It was the same kind of itch he got when he needed a drink, or when he missed Isaac's touch on his body, and the way they'd entwined in too-narrow beds.

Miss Comet lifted her chin. "Would you like me to ask again tomorrow, after you've thought it over?"

Landan pushed aside memories of Isaac. He cleared his dry throat. "Who said I was this Landan fellow anyway? Maybe I'm an impostor."

"The editor of the *Goldstone Times* described you perfectly, and said he'll vouch for you entirely."

Damn all writers, he thought without rancor. Damn the people who found out your secrets and then told them to the world. Maybe even damn the liquor that loosened his mouth, made him admit stories of the war he should have kept quiet.

Grudgingly he said, "I don't come cheap. And I'll need an advance to pay for my room and incidentals."

"Money's not a problem," she said. "But there won't be any drinking on this journey, Captain. I need you sober and committed to the job."

She put a small silk bag on the table between them. Inside it, Landan found a fistful of shiny silver dollars. It was more than he'd seen in a long while. He wondered how rich she really was.

"No drinking on the job," he agreed, and took the bag.

But the night was still young, and the job several hours away.

~ ~ ~

Morning came like an artillery blast to the brain. Landan's skull and body both ached as he glared at the generous breakfast in front of him.

Eggs, toast, bacon and hotcakes. He wanted to vomit. He didn't trust himself to speak and so kept his mouth shut while Miss Comet prattled on to an elderly couple at the next table. She had descended the hotel staircase dressed in a riding skirt, tailored green jacket, high leather boots and a hat wide enough to cast a shadow on an entire herd of cattle. Landan thought it was ludicrous. Riding was hot, sweaty work, and she sure was a city slicker if she thought she'd be comfortable in that get-up.

Still, he wasn't one to talk much about clothing. His only pair of trousers had worn thin at the knees, his shirt stank to his own nose, and there was a hole in the toe of his left boot. He'd shaved and doused water over his hair, and was as presentable as he intended to be, but he was well aware that he was one shabby, sorry-looking companion.

To hell with it, he thought to himself. She hadn't hired him for his handsome looks.

After breakfast, they went directly to the stable where she'd already made arrangements. For him, she had hired a gray gelding with a streak of white between his eyes. For Miss Comet herself, a lad brought out a sleek brown pony in high spirits. Trailing both was a sad-looking brown mule already loaded up with food, water, oats, bedrolls, two tweed suitcases, a bright yellow carpetbag and three sturdy hatboxes.

"What's all this?" Landan asked, perplexed.

Miss Comet said, "One must always be prepared."

Landan scratched the mule's ears, commiserating silently, and then double-checked the saddle and straps on his gelding. Miss Comet mounted her pony with the boy's assistance and sat serenely until he was done. She showed no trouble in her saddle as they rode down the street and past the town cemetery. The sun was relentlessly bright even at such an early hour, the rolling landscape dry and dusty.

"I love travel," she said once they were past the town limits. "It tests the soul, scours the body. Makes a person new again. Don't you think so, Captain?"

He'd done a fair bit of traveling in his time, and nothing had made him new. He was impure, through and through, had known it since he was a boy. Couldn't be cured.

"I'm not a captain any longer," he said. "Just call me Sam."

"'Captain' sounds so much more interesting," she said. "My husband served in the war as a captain, too."

Landan's gaze dropped to her gloved hands. He hadn't seen a ring on her during dinner.

"When you wear expensive jewelry, people try to steal it," Miss Comet observed. "Like those gentlemen following us even now."

He had noticed the signs, but was surprised she had, too. Two men on horseback about a quarter-mile back. Thieves who'd marked her back in town as an easy target. "I figured they'll wait until we stop for a rest, circle around, cut us off."

Miss Comet sighed. "Violence is such a blunt instrument."

Instead of waiting to be ambushed they took to a small ridge, waited for their followers, and scared off the scruffy would-be thieves with some well-aimed shots. Landan was impressed with Miss Comet's grace and composure in the face of armed robbery. Later they ate lunch by an arroyo. He wanted to scoff at the delicate cheese sandwiches she'd brought, but the pickle relish and thick slices of bread were so damn tasty he ate two of them, then a third.

"You're a woman of rare skills," he admitted. Isaac would have liked her, even though he shied away from most women.

"I try my best," she said modestly.

He fed and watered both horses and the mule, which was gazing off at the horizon as if thinking of all the interesting things it could be doing other than hauling luggage. Miss Comet did her personal business out of his sight, which was only proper. While she was gone he dared a nip or two from his flask. For medicinal purposes, nothing else. When Miss Comet came back he saw that she'd loosened her high collar in deference to the heat. He could see a small cut on her neck like the kind he sometimes got when he shaved. He'd seen women before with beards and tiny mustaches, and always felt bad for their misfortune.

"Tell me about this boy you're looking for," he said when they started riding again.

"Kevin is his name. He was one of many young boys orphaned by disease in Massasoit. We took him into our home for children and matched him with a family out here looking for a son. He's twelve years old now, and James and I have received no response to our last two letters."

James. Her husband, he guessed. A rich man who would have been given a commission to serve in the war, not earned it like Landan had. He said, "Just two letters? Hardly seems like a reason to come all this way."

Miss Comet adjusted her hat. "We take our responsibilities very seriously at the Hartvern Home. I have a personal, lifelong interest in each one of our wards. I can't send children west without following up on their safety and happiness."

He resented the implication that the territory was the kind of place where young boys would be neglected or abused. Then again, he'd seen it enough; orphan boys and girls sent from cities to work on ranches and farms, their prospects for education and achievement shunted into years of backbreaking work.

The desert landscape became more rugged and green, the cactuses and shrubs giving way to oaks and acacias, then to junipers and ponderosa pines. From switchback turns on the trail they could see Goldstone in the arid valley below. The heat was still intense, even as the forest grew around them. Miss Comet stripped off her gloves and loosened her jacket. She began singing a tune that he gradually recognized from his days at East Point:

> Eighty and nine with their captain
> Rode on the enemy's track
> Rode in the gray of the morning
> Nine of the ninety came back

"You shouldn't be singing about death," he chided.

"And you shouldn't be carrying a liquor flask," she replied.

He wanted to reach for it right then and take a swig, just out of spite. But he didn't. "You don't have the words right."

"There are many variations," she said. "I learned this one in the hospital, after James's injury."

He'd figured her husband as the type to stay behind enemy lines, not brave the front. "What kind of injury?"

"Bullet through the right femur."

One sip of whiskey, that was all he wanted. Landan wiped his forehead. "Did he lose the leg?"

"No. We saved it. I know some medicine on my own, and he had a most excellent surgeon."

Of course a rich man would be able to afford a private physician to coax him through the horrors and hazards of a war hospital. Landan had visited men in wards, smelled the piss and shit and pus, seen the pile of amputated limbs out by the pigpen. At night, on the winds that swept through the desert and up into mountains, he could hear the cries of anguish and anger, of lives slowly being wrung out of suffering bodies. A rich officer in an army hospital would have his own private room, and nurses with clean clothes, and food that wasn't crawling with flies or maggots.

"I think the most fascinating thing—" Miss Comet started to say, but then her pony let out a shriek, reared up on its hind legs, and whipped into a turn. With a yelp she grabbed for the reins. Gravity and force had the best of her, and she was hurled to the ground like a rag doll.

Landan turned his own horse from the ruckus before it too could panic, and pulled his pistol to face whatever threat faced them—rattlesnake, probably, something that slithered off the path into the green forest and was gone before he could get off a shot. Heart hammering wildly, he slid out of his saddle to the ground beside Miss Comet's body. She was loosely curled on her side, her hat skewed and crushed, her dark hair knocked loose. Not dead, but barely breathing.

With a start he realized her hair was a wig—a fine weave, expensive, but now so askew that any passing stranger would see the tight skull cap beneath it. He reached toward it, worried about bumps to her head, but just then she drew in a sharp breath and bolted upright into a sitting position. Her arms flailed in panic.

"You're fine!" he told her, grabbing her hands. "Just fine!"

She gasped for air, her gaze wild. "My horse! A snake—"

"It's gone."

Her hands went to her head, and panic washed through her expression. Landan's gaze shifted downward, as he intended to give her time to fix herself, but then he saw something more surprising then her wig. Her breasts had shifted. One was riding high, pointed toward the sky. The other had lurched left, toward the trees, in a way unlike any breast he'd ever seen.

"You're…" Landan started to say, but he couldn't finish the thought. He thought of her big hands, the cut on her neck. The fastidious insistence on grooming and apparel. Blood rushed to his face as puzzle pieces came together. He sat back, then climbed to his feet.

"I'll get the horses," he croaked out.

While his back was turned, she hurried off into the trees. He concentrated on collecting and calming the animals, for even the mule needed some settling down.

"Captain Landan!" That was Miss Comet's voice, from behind the solid brown trunk of a pine. Her voice was steadier than he trusted his own to be. "If you could pass me my yellow saddlebag and green suitcase, I would be much obliged."

Her sleeved arm extended expectantly. He got the luggage untied with trembling fingers, then handed both off.

"Are you injured?" he asked.

"Of course not," she replied.

He rubbed his face with his gloved hand, took a nip from his flask. His head hurt just as surely as if he'd hit it on a brick wall. He'd seen boys pretending to be women just for the fun of it. He'd seen girls in boy's clothing sneaking into the camps, sometimes for romantic trysts, sometimes so they could fight in the trenches. But it was safe to say that in all his years he'd never seen a man so determined—or confused—as this one.

It was a good hour before Miss Comet emerged again—impeccably attired, breasts and hair properly restored. Her expression—his? Landan wondered—was resolute.

"It's none of your business," she said, "but as a child, I was seriously disfigured in a tragic accident. It's nothing I like to speak of but it did leave me with certain…irregularities. I would appreciate your discretion and silence on the matter."

He couldn't quite hide his disbelief.

"If it's a problem for you, you're welcome to return to Goldstone. I can continue on my own."

"No," he said. "I said I'd do it. We'd best get going."

She gave him a narrow look, as if judging his worthiness, and then reached for her reins.

The rest of the afternoon passed without conversation. By dusk they were still ten miles out from Kelly's Pass, and the horses needed rest as much as their riders did. On the banks of a slick stream Landan got the animals watered, fed and groomed. With the sun below the trees, the canyons were cool and scenic around them. A man could live out here in peace forever, he thought wistfully. Why couldn't Isaac see that, appreciate it as the truth? He tried hard not to look at Miss Comet, who was cooking up tinned meat over a small campfire. Every brief glance had him studying the curve of her jaw, the thin blade of her nose, the way her wig was set just so.

"Captain Landan, it's rude to stare," she said tersely.

"I'm not—" Landan wrinkled his nose. "I'm just surprised."

"That a woman could be so cruelly disfigured, and struggle all her life to overcome it?"

"Something like that."

"Fate is cruel. Surely you learned that on the battlefield."

When it was dark they bedded down in thin blankets with the stars gloriously spread from one side of the sky to the other. For thousands of years men had been weaving love stories and adventure tales from dots connected into pictures, but all Landan could see were random pinpricks of indifferent light. He wondered, not for the first time since they'd made camp, if he was in danger of any kind. Miss Comet had already proved herself to be deceptive. For all he knew she'd lured him out here to kill him, and there was no child to be sought after at the Circle W.

"Captain, I can hear your silly thoughts all the way over here," she said from her blankets.

He shifted the saddlebag he was using as a pillow. "You're a mind-reader, too, is that it?"

"You deny it?"

"I can't deny that I'm a little unsettled. Does your husband know? Has he seen you—"

She raised a sharp hand. "Of course he's aware of my tragic history."

He bit back a surge of nastiness. "I've seen tragedies, Miss Comet. Soldiers gone blind, or their eardrums burst, or legs blown off, paralyzed, shell-shocked, maimed, no hands, no arms, boys who'll never grow old, mothers who lost all their children, fathers burying their firstborns and secondborns and last sons, and with all due respect, you don't look like any tragedy at all. Whatever story you want to tell, you tell it. But don't expect my sympathy."

She was silent for a long time. He felt bad about losing his temper, but not so bad that he could form an apology.

"You're right," came her reply, eventually, in the thin voice of someone long exhausted. "My ploy is inappropriate around a man of your history. Around anyone, I suppose. My apologies."

The saddlebag was digging into the back of his skull. He pushed it aside, opted for the hard ground instead. "I suppose it doesn't come up very often."

"Not when I'm careful." She rustled in her blankets. When he glanced over, he saw her watching him by the red light of the campfire coals. Her eyes were wide and solemn.

"I trust you with my secret," she said.

The last time he'd been in this forest, it had been with Isaac. The last time he'd gazed up at the stars, it had been with Isaac's heat and weight against his left side. Then morning had come, with such a terrible argument. Three months it had been, and the wound was still festering.

He rolled away from her. "I give you my word."

When he woke at sunup she was gone, but he heard the sounds of her morning ablutions just down the dry creekbed. He fixed breakfast and coffee for the two of them. She returned, looking as pert and well-dressed as any high society lady off to a day of shopping and afternoon tea.

"Good morning," she said.

"Morning," he returned.

Her gaze was speculative. "When we get back to Goldstone, you should invest in a new wardrobe. I think you would clean up just fine if you put your mind to it."

"Putting on airs isn't a priority out here."

"It is if you ever hope to attract a wife."

Landan swallowed the last of his coffee and studied the bottom of the tin cup. He wished he'd put more whiskey in it. Funny, how he'd passed through the worst days of his life stone-cold sober, but now he needed some fortitude to get through even such a beautiful morning.

"Captain Landan," Miss Comet said gently. "You deserve love. Everyone does."

He took the cup to the stream and rinsed it out. "You wanted to go to the Circle W. Let's go."

They made it to the ranch while the sun was still halfway toward noon. The Circle W was a generous spread of land near the Mokumne River, the rounded mountains providing a stunning backdrop. Once upon a time, Landan wouldn't have minded a place like it for himself—a place to raise cattle, to have a bed that wasn't a blanket on hard ground, to eat regular hot meals with someone he loved. They passed a corral of men wrangling horses before reaching a log house nestled in a copse of pines. The rancher's wife, Mrs. Bailey, met them at the door wearing a plain blue dress and long apron.

"My stars!" she said, her face full of wonder "It's you, isn't it? Miss Comet! Kevin said that one day you'd come visit. He said you'd show up on the doorstep all fancy, with a very nice hat, and that you'd have your handsome husband with you."

Her gaze shifted to Landan and scrunched up a little in surprise. Clearly he didn't match her expectations.

"Mrs. Bailey," Miss Comet said, offering her hand. "So very nice to meet you in person. This is Captain Landan, who escorted me from Goldstone."

Landan tipped his hat. "I'll let you two fine ladies see to your business," he said, and didn't even trip over the word ladies.

"Business!" Mrs. Bailey put her hand over her mouth in distress. "Oh, Kevin. You're here to see Kevin. But he's not here. My husband Hank set off just last week to bring him home."

"Bring him home from where?" Miss Comet asked, her confusion clear.

"From up north, in Flagpole," Mrs. Bailey said. "That's where we think he is. Traveling in the company of Mr. Whitney Waltman, the Amazing Undead Author."

~ ~ ~

Landan really hadn't planned on sitting down to tea. He'd figured on leaving Miss Comet and Mrs. Bailey to their talk, getting the animals watered, and then heading back to Goldstone for the pleasure of a week-long drunk in the same hotel he'd left behind. But the name Whitney Waltman made his heart pound an extra few beats. The famous poet, balladeer and journalist had been making headlines back east for almost twenty years with verses that shocked, enraged, delighted. As a military cadet, Landan had stashed his contraband copy of Waltman's work in a secret cubbyhole in his desk. Around campfires he'd recited one memorized verse after another to Isaac, who couldn't believe a man could write about illicit love and hedonism in such a way without getting run out of town by church folk.

"Back east, the hedonists outnumber the church folk," Landan had told him.

Waltman wrote not only about pleasure but also of the common lives of carpenters, laundresses, steelworkers, shipbuilders, teachers, and working folk of every ilk; he talked about cities rising out of meadows and forests, of ships that forged rivers bearing passengers, freight, the building blocks of a new nation; he spoke of longing, grief, ambition, tragedy. Landan had felt feverish for days after finishing the book. Other men brought bibles to war; he brought Waltman. But he'd lost his copy, his saddlebag, and nearly his life at the Battle of Ashville. Not until he met Isaac did he think he could share those words. They'd made a special trip to the bookstores of Elizabeth City and found a worn but serviceable copy. Around campfires, with only the trees and owls and stars as witnesses, he'd murmured the words against Isaac's throat and chest, and Isaac repeated them back like prayers.

"—I suppose that it's my fault," Miss Comet was saying, and the admission brought him back from reverie into Mrs. Bailey's sitting room. "I told Kevin he could take any one volume from my husband's library for the train trip out here, and he selected Mr. Waltman."

Mrs. Bailey fiddled with her blue tea cup. "It's not that we don't appreciate literature, ma'am. But perhaps that was too…explicit for a boy his age?"

"Nonsense," Miss Comet said, without rancor. "At Hartvern House, our children start reading classical tragedies before they learn to tie their shoes. We encourage a thorough understanding of the world."

Mrs. Bailey sighed. "Kevin heard that Mr. Waltman was speaking in San Geraldo. It's his final tour, given his recent health calamities. Kevin begged to go. That's almost four hundred miles away! After we refused, he slipped out his window and ran away. Hank brought him back two days later. Then Kevin learned Mr. Waltman would be in Auraria. He jumped on a train like a hobo and got all the way to the theater doors before Hank caught him and marched him home. Three days ago, Kevin found out that Mr. Waltman would be speaking tonight in Flagpole. He was gone before we could talk sense into him. So you see, Miss Comet, I couldn't answer your letters. I didn't want to lie and say everything was fine. The child is a firefly, always flitting off to the horizon. But I never imagined you'd come all this way to check on him!"

"I have a responsibility," Miss Comet replied. "Clearly you are loving parents, even if you underestimate the power of literature on a young man's mind. When I was Kevin's age, I hitchhiked with a gang of camel thieves across an entire desert to hear the poet Gibran speak on the emperor's birthday."

Mrs. Bailey's hand rose to her throat. "A girl so young! You could have been killed! Or molested!"

"To hear Gibran, one should be willing to risk more than life itself." Miss Comet put down her cup. "Now, if you'll allow us some time to freshen up, the Captain and I must be on our way to Flagpole."

"What?" Landan asked, startled.

Miss Comet rose gracefully. "We'll have to leave right now if we're going to see Mr. Waltman's engagement."

"I didn't say I'd take you to Flagpole," he protested.

"Of course you will," she said, with a sweet smile.

~ ~ ~

Of course he did. Not just for the money, of which she promised more, and not out of fear for her safety. He didn't believe the desert story—camel thieves, indeed—but she was resourceful enough to follow the well-traveled roads to Flagpole with little if any trouble. He went for the same reason a twelve-year-old boy climbed out his window. The famous author, holding court. The Amazing Undead Author, mocking his own mortality while simultaneously lurching toward it. Landan knew a thing or two about Death, and how quickly it could rush over a soul when least expected.

He denied any interest at all in Waltman, of course.

"Read one author, you've read them all," he said to Miss Comet as they rode north. The mule, which seemed to have gotten its hopes up back at the Bailey ranch, trod along on its tether with an occasional bray of discontent.

"You break my heart," Miss Comet replied. "That's like saying every sunrise is identical, every snowflake from the sky. Every drop of precious liquor."

He hid a smirk. "Whiskey's different than gin, and gin's different than bourbon, but they all do the same job."

Miss Comet adjusted her hat. "Make one insensate? Or open a mind to possibilities?"

Now she was quoting Waltman, sonnet twelve. He said, "If you're such a big proponent, you should try a drop or two."

She replied, "I drink plenty. When appropriate, and not while doing my job."

The words made him cross. He hadn't touched his flask today, but another snide remark and he'd reconsider his temperance. Landan wondered if any man could accompany her on an extended journey without the benefit of a nip or two.

"Why didn't your husband make the trip with you?" he asked.

"If you were married, would you insist on accompanying your wife everywhere?"

"I'm not likely to get married, ma'am."

"You could use a partner," she observed.

He was trying hard to keep Isaac out of his thoughts. It was unlikely, but not impossible, that he would have heard of Whitney Waltman's scheduled appearance in Flagpole. That slight flare of possibility made Landan simultaneously hopeful and sick to his stomach. What would he do, if he looked across the room and saw Isaac in the crowd—slim and sinewy, his hands jammed shyly in his pockets, his cornsilk hair slicked back for the occasion?

He realized the horses had stopped at the base of a narrow wooden bridge. The river flowed lazily beneath them. Miss Comet was looking at him in amusement.

"What's that?" he asked.

"You were lost in reverie," Miss Comet asked. "Who's the lucky lady?"

"There's no goddamn lucky lady," Landan snapped, and something flashed across Miss Comet's face.

"I see," she said, with a lift of her eyebrows. Then she nudged her horse onto the bridge and he had only the back of her head to consider.

Hurriedly he urged his gelding to catch up. Hoof beats on the bridge sounded like thunder, and it wasn't until they were across that he got to say, "There's nothing to see about it—"

"Captain Landan," she said, stopping her horse. She raised her hand in a forestalling motion and gave him a look of genuine sympathy. "I am the least likely person on this planet to condemn any kind of love between two consenting adults. You need not worry about me gossiping, spreading rumors, or otherwise sabotaging your reputation. I remain your friend, and would be honored to be your confidante, but simply say the word and I shall never mention it again."

He gazed at her hard.

"Never mention it again," he said gruffly.

She turned her pony down the path.

Christ, he needed a drink.

~ ~ ~

Other men might have been relieved by having their darkest secret pulled into the light and acknowledged by an acquaintance of less than forty-eight hours. Landan felt raw and exposed, as if he'd been stripped and staked out to die a long death in the middle of the desert. The sun was too bright, his saddle suddenly uncomfortable, the gelding just a little too fast despite his attempts to rein him back. He could barely eat his lunch. He drank water from his canteen but it tasted like grit, and he had to spit it out or be sick.

Miss Comet said nothing about his mental state, if she even observed it at all. She was too busy mangling a new set of verses:

With bray of the trumpet and roll of the drum
And keen ring of the bugle, the soldiers come
Sharp clank the steel swords, the bridle-chains ring
And foam from red nostrils, the wild chargers sing

"Cavalry," he finally said. "It's not soldiers, it's cavalry. Scabbards, not swords. And the wild chargers fling. There's not much singing when you're attacking the enemy."

"Are you quite sure?"

He'd heard the song in camps, in public houses, in beer halls after the war. He was quite sure.

"I'm thinking of collecting a series of ballads into a printed volume," she said. "You would be a valuable resource. Have you ever thought of becoming an author?"

"The only good labor is physical labor," he replied.

"I think Mr. Waltman would disagree with that," Miss Comet said.

"Then why did he write so many verses about the common working man?"

"I thought you hadn't read his work."

Damn it. "Just might have heard of him, that's all."

"Captain Landan, I expect a man of your caliber to be honest about literature, even if you can't be honest about anything else."

"I'm goddamned honest!" he protested. "About the things that need honesty. About things that won't get you strung up, or tarred and feathered and run out of town. This isn't Massasoit. It's not a forgiving place."

"They wouldn't forgive you for reading Waltman?"

"Yes!" he snapped. "No. You make a man all confused!"

She gave him a sunny smile. "When I can, yes."

If he liked women in a romantic way, he would have liked her. But then he remembered that she wasn't a woman at all, was something else entirely, and he had to turn his attention to the trail.

"Captain Landan," she said a moment later. "Surely you've heard 'The Ballad of William Jane'."

He had to think hard on that one. It was an older song, back from the wars between Cardyr and Kilvemi. A young wife dressed up as a man to join her husband in battle, but was unable to save his life. Unmasked by her fellow soldiers, she was discharged and ostracized. Later she died saving the same regiment of men who'd rejected her.

"It's just a song," he said.

"Songs and poetry tell truths."

"They give you hope that you don't deserve."

She shook her head. "They shed light on the human condition."

"The human condition that made you and me wrong?" he demanded. "That makes us live in shame of being ourselves?"

She stopped dead on the road. Landan noticed, turned. Her face was curiously hard, nearly fierce.

"Whatever I am, I'm not ashamed of it," she said.

He felt his face blush. "That's not what I meant."

"It's exactly what you meant."

Landan nudged his gelding back into motion and didn't answer her.

Soon they reached a junction with a broad road heading north toward Flagpole, and in the next few hours they passed settlers in wagons, men driving stubborn mules, a group of indigenous people carrying buckets on their shoulders, three farm girls with pigtailed hair, six miners with pickaxes, and any number of itinerant cowboys, hoboes, peddlers and madmen. Landan tried not to think about what secrets each might be holding close—who they loved, what they were afraid of, the inconsistencies in their hearts and bodies. In the golden light of late afternoon he and Miss Comet reached the town itself. Flagpole was the largest town for a hundred miles around, an epicenter of trade and logging and industry, with a railroad running along its main street. The best hotel was the Monte Vista and they went there directly.

The hotel was surrounded by a number of restaurants and shops. Directly across the street was a grand theater with an arched marquee and printed playbills: MR. WHITNEY WALTMAN, THE NOTED AUTHOR, IN PERFORMANCE TONIGHT ONLY! He tried to ignore it while he unloaded Miss Comet's baggage from the long-suffering mule.

Miss Comet asked, "Would you care to be my guest for the show tonight?"

"No, ma'am," he said. Because he'd thought on it, and thought again, and nothing good could come of it. He'd been a fool to think otherwise. "I'm going to find my own room and retire early."

In the diminishing light, with the bustle of folks heading home for the night or heading out for entertainment, she paid him his wages. Then she reached deeply into her carpetbag and withdrew a slim volume. "Here. If you haven't read it, you'll find it quite interesting. If you have, maybe a refresher is in order."

It was Waltman's collection. Landan took it in puzzlement. "You just happen to have a copy?"

"I asked Mrs. Bailey to loan me Kevin's copy," she said. "I thought perhaps I'd have it inscribed. But like a man dying of thirst, you have more need of it."

A bellboy in a smart blue uniform came out to carry Miss Comet's bags. She gave him a brilliant smile, warned him to be extra careful with her belongings, and swept past the doorman into the dim interior of the hotel. Just like that she was gone from Landan's sight, with no final words of advice or goodwill. He wondered if he'd earned her enmity forever by speaking the honest truth. That was his life in a nutshell: missed opportunities, broken relations, regret. Hers would be just one more name added to the list he carried in his heart.

He took the animals to the stable, bought himself the biggest bottle of whiskey he could find, and checked into the Weatherford Hotel. He put the whiskey and the copy of Waltman on the bedside table, and then he considered the best way to start his week-long binge.

~ ~ ~

Landan dreamed he was back in uniform. Muddy, bloody trenches rose around him, blocking his vision, collapsing in so that he couldn't breathe, couldn't claw his way free. Then he was running in a cold morning fog, isolated, cut off from his men, aware only of his own harsh breathing and the impact of bullets into flesh: the soft, unmistakable horror of it, small thumps as invisible human bodies were pierced and wounded. He couldn't see his men but he could hear them dying. He dreamt of Isaac in uniform, which was untrue to history, and he dreamt of weeping women holding their mortally wounded husbands. You couldn't hold onto a person tight enough to forestall fate.

He dreamed of the morning he'd tossed Waltman's book into the campfire, the capstone of a spectacular argument with Isaac that had nothing to do with poetry and everything to do with Isaac's desire to visit the east. To frequent the beer halls and saloons where a man could hold another man's hand, where he could be affectionate before strangers who shared the same predilections. Frustration swept over Landan like hot oil as he tried to make Isaac understand. That world was elusive, precarious, left a man open to rumors of scandal. It was fine if you were a dandy poet who lived hand to mouth. For a man who had to hold down a good job, it was too dangerous. Did Isaac want to be beaten, killed? It had happened to soldiers. It had nearly happened to Landan himself.

In the dream, Isaac ignored all of Landan's words. Beside them, the fire that consumed Waltman's book rose up, parted the clouds, and scoured the sky. The flames shot back down with heat that broiled away Landan's skin and all the bones in his outstretched arms. The roar of artillery surrounded him like thunder and diminished him to dust. There was nothing, then, no sound or feeling or sense of place in the world; nothing so complete he was surely dead, and it was a surprise when the morning sun woke him.

He lurched upright, heart pounding, sweat pooling out of him. The copy of Waltman's book was on the bedside table where he'd left it.

So was the whiskey, untouched.

He scrubbed his face with dry hands. Picked up the book and read a random line: *Clear and sweet is my soul, and clear and sweet is all that is not my soul.*

Landan kept reading. The clean, clear pages soothed his fingers, made his heart slowly calm. Gradually he reclined back in the bed with the pillow bunched under his head. When his stomach rumbled he got a boy to go down to the restaurant and fetch him some biscuits and ham for breakfast, but other than that and some necessary business with the slop jar, he didn't move off the bed. The good people of Flagpole went about their business without his assistance and very nearly without his notice, aside from the clop of horses in the street, the sidewalk conversations that rose to his open windows, the piano music coming out of the music hall on the corner. Despite it all he remained immersed. Slits of sunlight moved across the small room, warming his legs and then his arms and finally his face, but he rolled onto his side and kept reading.

Gradually he became aware that dusk was coming on, and that he was sore from lying on a lumpy mattress all day, and that the pianist across the street was playing that goddamned "Campside Traces." On unsteady feet he crossed to the window and sucked in fresh air. Far down the street he could see the arched marquee of the theater where Whitney Waltman had so recently performed.

The pianist finished up his song. In the relative piece and quiet, someone knocked on Landan's door.

Miss Comet was dressed in fine purple dress with a lace throat and lace collars. Her wig was arranged in a spiral of curls, and expertly applied makeup made her eyes look deep and velvety. Standing with her was a neatly groomed boy nervously tugging on his collar, and a tall rancher looking uncomfortable in a suit.

"Captain Landan," Miss Comet said briskly. "May I introduce Mr. Hank Bailey and his son Kevin?"

The men shook hands. Kevin mumbled a hello, and shuffled and scratched like he had ants in his pants.

"Boy, you stay still," Bailey said, sounding both fond and exasperated in equal parts. He made a move to slick down Kevin's unruly hair, and the boy ducked away.

"We're going to be late to the show!" Kevin said.

Landan gazed at the three of them in bewilderment.

"What show?"

"Mr. Waltman," Bailey said with a shrug. "Miss Comet here, she convinced me it would be good for the boy's education."

"But that was all last night," Landan said.

"Mr. Waltman was delayed by an inconveniently unreliable locomotive," Miss Comet announced. "The performance was rescheduled for tonight. I have an extra ticket, if you're interested."

Reflexively he said, "I don't have anything to wear."

Bailey said, a little ruefully, "That's what I said."

"The tailor across the street has been told to expect you within the next quarter hour. He'll take care of all your needs." Miss Comet lifted the half-full bottle of whiskey from the bedside table. "I suggest you not indulge in this until afterward."

"I can't," Landan said, and it was unbearable: the thought of putting on fine clothes, sitting in a darkened auditorium, hearing the author himself speak words that Landan had held so intimately in his hands all day long. The prospect of Isaac being there. "Miss Comet, thank you, but I can't."

"We have to go or we're going to be late!" Kevin complained.

"I'll be departing on the morning train," Miss Comet continued, sounding unconcerned about whatever Landan decided. "I leave in your care the horses, as well as that very unhappy mule. Do with them what you please. I would like to have Kevin's book back, of course. He'll want it autographed."

Landan nodded toward the table, where the book and whiskey sat side by side.

Miss Comet looked over, nodded, and then said, "Come now, gentlemen, off we go." She ushered Kevin out toward the hallway. His father followed, pulling uncomfortably on his collar. Miss Comet made no move to collect Waltman's volume but instead waited until only she and Landan remained.

Somberly she said, "He's down there, Sam."

Goosebumps rose on Landan's arms. "Who?"

"Whoever you're looking for," she said. "Whatever his name proves to be, whatever appearance he might take. If you can imagine it, you can find it. Whatever decisions you've made wrongly in the past, the future is yet unwritten. Do with it what you will. Without shame, without regret."

She closed the door with a gentle snick, and just like that was gone again.

Landan went back to his window. The light of street lamps flickered yellow, and gay music pounded out of the music halls and saloons, and he thought he could hear Waltman's voice beneath it all, murmuring encouragement.

When he left the room a few minutes later he took the book with him but left behind the whiskey. Where he was going, he only needed one of them.

Author's notes

1. Surely Mr. Waltman needs no introduction to this audience.
2. Occasionally copies of the manuscript *Diana Comet and the Camel Thieves* appear in auction catalogs or the bright pixels of eBay. These invariably turn out to be fakes.
3. Sam Landan and Isaac Walter first met on a cattle drive near Brokeback Mountain; the Walters, of course, are an important family in Tony Kushner's award-winning play *Angels in America*. The Weatherford Hotel in Flagstaff, Arizona, has a quite lovely balcony where writers can congregate over beer, popcorn, and a view of downtown.
4. The author is indebted to the book *American War Ballads, 1725-1865,* ed. by George Cary Eggleston, published in 1889.

A resident of San Francisco, **Simon Sheppard** is the author of *Sodomy!; Hotter Than Hell and Other Stories; Kinkorama; In Deep: Erotic Stories;* and *Sex Parties 101*, and editor of the Lambda-Award-winning *Homosex: Sixty Years of Gay Erotica,* and of *Leathermen*. His work has also appeared in over 300 anthologies, including seventeen editions of the *Best Gay Erotica* series and several editions of *The Best American Erotica*. He hangs out at simonsheppard.com.

BAREBACKING

Simon Sheppard

In the beginning, you didn't mean to. Not at all. But there you were, with a condom around your rapidly deflating dick and a beautiful brown Indian man in your bed. The Indian's hole was, as usual, tight, and the guy had already told you that he'd thought you two had fucked raw before, a few months back. Which wasn't true. Whatever.

You were virtually certain your partner was negative; you knew damn well that you were. You peeled off the condom and threw it on the floor. Squirting a little more lube on your dick, you began sliding your hard-on against the man's warm, welcoming ass. Your cock instantaneously grew hard, harder than it had been all night.

It had been so many years, so long since you'd had unprotected sex. The Indian guy turned over on his stomach, the way he always liked to get fucked.

It was easy, amazingly easy, to slide inside. For the first time since you'd started screwing the guy, it seemed like there was no resistance, no fight. *This is so wrong,* you thought, but that didn't stop you from sliding all the way in and staying there. Considering the number of times you had fucked the fellow—a married man whose wife (pronounced, in the Indian fashion, "vife," providing a little cross-cultural thrill) was often out of town—this time felt surprisingly unfamiliar. Luxurious, that was the word for it. *Luxurious.*

You raised yourself up on your extended arms and looked down at the broad brown back. Sliding your dick in and out, in and out, you couldn't believe how totally, absolutely, fantastically great it felt.

Well, strictly speaking, that wasn't true. You *could* believe it, easily. It was, after all, how sex had once been supposed to feel, but at the same time it was as if the two of you had a dirty little secret, one neither of you would ever tell.

The Indian man had always been, in fact, a great, hungry bottom once his hole had loosened up. But now, skin on skin, there had been no initial tightness, no gradual ramping up of pleasure, and it took an effort of will not to come too soon. You would have liked to switch positions, to get the guy on his back, look down at his handsome face, kiss him. But it was what it was: The guy didn't kiss, and he preferred it from behind. So you pounded away, enjoying what surely must be a once-only raw fuck.

You were so very, very happy.

"You're not going to come inside me, right?"

"Of course not." You didn't mention you'd already felt yourself leaking precum deep inside his ass.

Pretty soon you sensed yourself reaching the point of no return. "I'm gonna come," you said, pulling your slick cock out of the well-used hole, looking down to watch the naked shaft sliding out. Without even having to touch yourself, you shot off all over the man's back, milky sperm on chocolate skin. You caught your breath, then rolled off your partner.

The just-fucked man turned over, a big smile on his face. His dark cock was still fully hard. He reached down and stroked himself till his nutsack, nearly black, tightened, pumping a big load out onto his belly.

"I loved when you fucked me," the man said. He had never used the word "love" before, in any context.

"Me, too," you said. "A lot." *I won't be doing that again,* you thought.

~ ~ ~

On your way home from the Indian's, the warm spring night seemed full of possibilities, the fragrance of night-blooming jasmine, for once, not cloying but absolutely perfect.

You stopped into an all-night donut place, braving the fluorescents, and got an apple fritter, still hot out of the oven, and a cup of coffee. The caffeine would keep you up till dawn, but that was okay; no work the next day. You bit into the smooth, sweet dough. Life was, indeed, good.

If you *had* done something dangerous, you had no idea what it had been.

~ ~ ~

A couple of weeks later, after you'd fucked your buddy a couple of more times, both without a condom, the Indian man's wife returned and further sex was, for the moment, off. Even your e-mails went unanswered.

For a week or so after that, unmanageably horny, you jacked off two or three times a day, but one night you decided to throw caution pretty much to the winds and answer an ad you'd seen online.

When your correspondent came over, he was even better looking than he'd looked in the photo he'd e-mailed—a very pleasant surprise. In his mid-twenties, the guy's face was pretty and unlined, his hair long and blondish, his handlebar mustache a waxed-up architectural achievement that framed his big, soft-looking lips.

"My name's Marc, with a 'c'," he said.

You hadn't even gotten to the bedroom when you started tearing each other's clothes off. Marc, sensing a belt-unbuckling problem, undid his own jeans and pulled them halfway down, revealing blue-checked boxers.

It was gratifying, when you reached down and groped through the cotton fabric, to discover that Marc's cock was small, thin, and very hard. Contrary to what you supposed you were supposed to prefer, you in fact had a thing for little dicks, and it was exciting to you that this lovely, slightly overweight young man had one.

Once Marc had thoroughly stripped down, his body plump, a bit furry, and otherwise desirable, it turned out that he also had an edible-looking, perfectly pink hole.

"Get on the bed, on your back, legs up," you said, and once Marc had done exactly that, hands grabbing ankles to keep his legs in the air, you hungrily dived right in. You really loved eating ass. Loved it past the point of explanation, of reason. Even at the height of your caution, you'd always rimmed asses—and, amazingly, had never suffered more than an upset tummy as a result of your passions.

After you'd sated yourself, you backed off, wiped your mouth, and spit-lubed your dick. This time, unlike the first bare fuck with the Indian, there was no hesitation. Marc had advertised for a raw fuck, and a raw fuck was what he was going to get.

He had warned you by e-mail that his hole was tight, but it wasn't, not really, though in any case, the extended rimming had prepped it well. Just a little prodding, and there it was: the feeling of skin sliding against skin. Well, it was against mucous membrane really, but that sounded a lot less romantic, and with your dick all the way inside Marc, your pubic bone pressing up against the boy's meaty ass, you weren't about to quibble over terminology.

"I'm getting a cramp in my leg," Marc said.

"Want to ride me, instead?"

"Sure."

You rearranged yourselves, Marc on top and straddling you, hole against hard cockhead. With one swift stroke, Marc lowered himself down on you, velvety hot softness enveloping your sensitive shaft.

You looked up at Marc's handsome face, at the cute mustache, the bright blue eyes, the skinny little dick oozing precum, and though you knew you were expected to keep fucking for a good long time, you realized you were, distressingly, already at the point of no return.

"Fuck, I'm going to come," you said.

If Marc was disappointed, he hid it well. "Go for it," he encouraged.

"Inside?" It had been prearranged, so you didn't really need permission, or if you did, it was your own permission to yourself.

"Yeah."

The spasms came from deep inside your balls, and they lasted for a long, long time, until you'd shot your entire load of sperm inside Marc's furry ass. Marc leaned over, allowing your dick to slide out of his butt. Though he'd said in his e-mails that he didn't kiss, Marc planted a surprising soft kiss on your mouth; that mustache felt great.

"Can I ask you a favor, Marc?"

"Sure, I think."

You'd been wanting to do this for a decade, more. "Let me eat your ass a little more."

When Marc was obligingly on all fours, you kneeled behind him and spread his asscheeks. As the hole relaxed, a stream of cum trickled out. You plunged your tongue against it, licking it up.

You jerked away with a shudder. *What the fuck am I doing?* you thought. Then you relaxed, snuggled your face against Marc's ass, and slurped some more.

~ ~ ~

Like any loss of virginity, you reflected, the first time had been the hardest. (Though okay, it hadn't really been the first time, since you had, many years ago, never used rubbers at all.)

But now that you had become almost accustomed to barebacking, nearly reconciled, now that you had found the very perfect Marc, the blond boy wasn't answering your e-mails; you sent four intentionally breezy notes suggesting you meet up again, then, not wanting to seem a pest, not wanting to feel any more rejected than necessary, gave up.

You once had an English boyfriend who'd taught you the phrase "In for a penny, in for a pound." Despite the vagaries of inflation, in this case it seemed appropriate.

A barebacking party was not, in your city, hard to find.

~ ~ ~

You hadn't been to a sex party for years, not, in fact, since you'd brought home a persistent case of scabies. So it was with a certain amount of trepidation that you made your way to the address specified in his invitation.

You were still unsure, actually, just what you'd be prepared to do once you got to the party. Unlike the Indian man and unlike Marc, the men at the party, you assumed, were more likely to fuck first, negotiate afterwards. Still, it might be interesting just to walk in the door....

When you paid your entrance fee and walked in the door—of a nicely furnished, middle-class house, as it happened, not some sleazy dive—you were pleasantly surprised to find a goodly variety of men already there, some already naked. Out of the couple of dozen guys, there were a few standard-issue gym bunnies, an unclothed older man with a thatch of unexpectedly sexy gray hair on his meaty chest, a young Asian man, Thai maybe, with beautiful eyes and a tight-fitting lycra wrestling singlet that showed off his hard dick. A prodigiously tattooed, skinny young blond guy with piercings everywhere, including his dick, a black man in Bermuda shorts, a bear or two. And you.

There was an air of sociability mixed with awkward expectancy; some of the men seemed to know each other well, while others hung around on the margins. Then one guy, obviously the organizer/host, announced that the door had been closed to newcomers and detailed the rules for the evening.

You hadn't realized till then what the set-up actually was—insufficient research, you supposed. The party was in fact a gang-bang, the tattooed boy the planned recipient of everyone else's loads. This was not only not a turn-on for you—you'd planned on a one-on-one, or a three-way at most—but a little worrisome, too. Fucking one ass without a rubber was one thing, plunging your cock into a reservoir of other men's cum, much of it no doubt infected, quite another. It was only after the festivities were already underway that you realized you might have asked to go first, thereby shortening your participation but allaying your fears. By then, though, one of the gym bunnies had groaningly popped a load inside the tattooed boy's ass, his cock quickly replaced by the gray-haired man's.

Meanwhile, some of the men were getting blown—fluffed for their upcoming fucks, no doubt, since oral sex to completion was not the main dish on the menu. The muscular man who had just finished fucking was headed your way, his cock still hard, at least probably a testament to the powers of Viagra.

"Drop your pants and I'll blow you," the muscular man said.

With a shock, you realized that you were the only one there who was still fully clothed. You unzipped your fly, took out your half-erect cock, and, when the well-built man was on his knees, slipped it between the guy's lips. It felt great, but you still weren't getting fully hard. You didn't think of yourself as a prude—far from it—but there was something slightly disconcerting about watching the older man, having come, pull out of the tattooed boy's slick, dripping hole, to be replaced mere seconds later by the Asian man. Hot, yes, but somehow not quite right.

"The bottom boy..." you began, speaking to no one in particular. The man sucking your cock paused for a minute, though, and looked up.

"Alex? He's a friend of mine. Bug-chaser. He came here for the gift. Been here before, actually, and it looks like he'll keep trying till he gets it."

That was it: enough. Too much, actually.

"Thanks for the head," you said, "but I think I'm going to split."

Taking care to seem casual, you made his way across the room, which already smelled of sweat, cum, and ass, and out the front door. You paused for a moment, until you heard the door being locked behind you, then headed home through the chill night air.

~ ~ ~

A couple of weeks after your abrupt departure from the party, you went to the clinic for the result of your HIV test.

Testing was always an anxiety-producing experience for you, but the results were, as expected, negative.

You hadn't barebacked since the party, hadn't had any kind of sex with anyone, actually. Marc, who'd warned you that he didn't play around all that often, hadn't even bothered to reply to your e-mails. And cruising Craigslist had turned out to be a frustrating pain in the ass. So you'd contented yourself, for the time being, with jacking off, sometimes to the point of soreness.

Then, one sunny morning, you got e-mail from your Indian friend:

Sorry I haven't got back in touch with you before, but I guess you understand. My wife is out of town again. Want to fuck me? "Bare" went unspoken, but implied.

You remembered the feeling of your unsheathed dick sliding into the caramel-colored man's soft hole, recalled licking your sperm from Marc's ass, thought about skinny little Alex getting gang-banged in a quest for HIV infection.

You reread the email.

Want to fuck me?

It took you a good long while to decide.

One of the original "New Narrative" writers of the 1980s, **Kevin Killian** lives in San Francisco. His most recent books include an edition of *Jack Spicer's Collected Poems*, a book of stories from City Lights Books (*Impossible Princess*) and a second volume of his *Selected Amazon Reviews*. A shorter version of "Repetition Island" was written for the exhibition of the same name, curated by Raimundas Malasauskas, and presented at the Centre Pompidou in Paris from July 7-12, 2010. The present expanded version first appeared in the Fall 2010 issue of the online journal *JMWW*.

Repetition Island

Kevin Killian

Monday. On Repetition Island plant life is scarce, so the owners ferry in caterers three times daily, and the crew's craft table is piled high with the fruits of the sea—lobster, shrimp, crab. While his body is still fit enough for the screen, young protag Mardi is making as much porn as he can. "Drink more milk," scream his directors, since milk is commonly thought to render the ass whiter, creamier. Mardi leads a rigorous screen life, and naps during breaks. Someone has to do it. Someone's got to bend over and spread his own cheeks, after milk breakfast, after milk lunch, milk enema, before his milk dinner. "Hello," says the asshole. "Both of us were object."

The other day he was trying to remember what life was like before he landed on Repetition Island, but thinking that way makes a boy crazy. It would be a sign of weakness, of an inability to hold your milk. "Would somebody please stick something up my butt and shut me up?" he cries humorously. The sun breaks through the clouds, on the beaches pink gravel shifts continuously, obliterating footprints, drying out trails of semen.

~ ~ ~

Tuesday. On Repetition Island plant life is scarce, but the producers ferry in caterers three times daily, and the crew's craft table is piled high with the fruits of the sea—lobster, shrimp, crab. "I'm into whitefish," Mardi offers, knowing somehow that this makes his listeners giggle: they are going to find a sexual meaning because his voice is so light, his lips so red. "Drink more milk," scream his directors, since milk is commonly thought to render the ass whiter, creamier. Today he is filming a sequence in which he is raped by a she-male partly dressed in the costume of a county guard. "Hello," says the asshole. "Both of us were object."

"Where are you from," whispers the she-male into his ear, as an enormous stiff organ pounds him onto the scratchy sheets of his cell bed. He doesn't reply. When he rises stiffly his chest and ribs are welted with flea-bites. Darn blanket. "Would somebody please stick something up my butt and shut me up?" he cries humorously. The sun breaks through the clouds, on the beaches pink gravel shifts continuously, obliterating footprints, drying trails of semen.

~ ~ ~

Wednesday. On Repetition Island plant life is scarce, so shade is currency, big stars get sturdy umbrellas and the rank and file like Mardi haul their canvas parasols from set to set. Breakfast is lobster, shrimp, crab. "Drink more milk," scream his directors, since milk is commonly thought to render the ass whiter, creamier. His dresser surveys his rear with churlish skepticism. "Yeah, you're a white boy, but I need snow color, not freckle color." "I hate fucking milk." Dresser slaps his butt, leaves handprint. "Are you up for a milk enema maybe?" Mardi hums the Kelis number they taught him for their musical episode. My milkshake brings all the boys to the yard, better than yours.

The other day he was trying to remember what life was like before he landed on Repetition Island, but thinking that way could make a boy crazy. It would be a sign of weakness, of an inability to hold your milk. "Would somebody please stick something up my butt and shut me up?" he cries humorously. The sun breaks through the clouds, on the beaches pink gravel shifts continuously, obliterating footprints, drying trails of milk.

~ ~ ~

Thursday. On Repetition Island plant life is scarce, but the crew's craft table is piled high with the fruits of the sea—lobster, shrimp, crab. Mardi chugs down a liter of milk as Mr. Guilfoyle looks on approvingly. Guilfoyle flips up Mardi's kilt in the back, inspects his merchandise. I've had my eye on you this summer, he says, or is Mardi imagining this part? Today his ass features in a sequence in which one hundred Scottish boys have been slain and heaped onto a ceremonial slab by Braveheart. "Hello," says the asshole. "Both of us were object."

Guilfoyle or one of them has his passport. When he came he knew some French and Spanish, but just as it builds up creaminess in the glutes, the milk diet's hell on language skills. In the afternoon his ass is built up into a planter in a greenhouse sequence in a porn noir. A leather daddy in leather trench coat parades up and down the orchids; Mardi and other flower boys watch his boots from upside down. The sun breaks through the clouds, on the beaches pink gravel shifts continuously, obliterating footprints, drying trails of semen.

~ ~ ~

Friday. The crew's craft table overflows with the fruits of the sea—lobster, shrimp, crab. Guilfoyle flips up Mardi's kilt in the back, inspects his merchandise, drawing a finger softened by mayonnaise up and down the boy's crack. Tall stars—and there are some tall performers on Repetition Island, though the majority are tiny twinks like Mardi—swear you can see from one end of the Island to the other, just popping up on your tiptoes. "What's it like being so big?" asks Mardi, trying to imagine. Tall star blinks, his cock swelling in Mardi's butt. "From loading dock on one end to lighthouse on the other, it's a company town, bro." Or did Mardi imagine this part? Dutifully, he submits to his milk enema at low tide, hands and knees in pebbled clear water. "Hello," says the asshole. "Both of us were object."

Guilfoyle or one of them has his passport. When he came he had some friends and spanking, but just as it builds up creaminess in the glutes. Milk is hard on relationships. In the afternoon his ass is built up into a planter in a greenhouse sequence in The Dick Slap. It's too white, the director calls out, and best boys rub down his butt with taffy and peatmoss. The sun breaks through the clouds, on the beaches pink gravel shifts continuously, obliterating footprints, drying trails of semen.

for Raimundas Malasauskas

Daniel Allen Cox is the author of the novel *Shuck,* shortlisted for a Lambda Literary Award, and *Krakow Melt,* also a finalist for a Lambda Literary Award and the Ferro-Grumley Award for LGBT Fiction. Both are published by Arsenal Pulp Press. A Turkish-language version of *Krakow Melt* is forthcoming from Istanbul-based publisher Altikirkbes. Daniel lives in Montreal.

DANIEL ALLEN COX

A Nose Commits Suicide

Daniel Allen Cox

It's a horrible substance to drown in, given my affinity for it. But after you read this, I think you'll understand why I performed the final, fatal inhalation. Technically, it's called "natricide"—death by violence to the nostrils—but I call it madness.

I did it for his body.

He would toss his hair, pretending to clear it from his eyes. I knew, however, that it was really to tease me closer with an explosion of oils, to seduce me with sebum. In the summer heat, his glands oozed everything I liked.

Then he'd tip his hair with gel and toss a little more, wafting chemicals my way and ruining the moment. I'd skulk off. Of course, he was hurt by my disdain for hair products, but kept tossing for other noses to hide his pain.

I was deceitful, too. When he wasn't looking, I'd position myself downwind and sniff. I couldn't get enough.

~ ~ ~

Betcha my family photo album looks nothing like yours.

Close-up of me as a baby nose: swaddled in blankets and my own newborn smell. My pores—which would later become thick marshes of blackheads—were still closed. I'm a shiny button, yet to be awakened by the rot and bloom of life. Oh, wait—there's a wrinkle. Perhaps an awareness that breast milk was only a few feet away…

Another shot, one of my favorites: a curious honker, growing but still little. Far too hungry for sugar. Jolly Rancher is a square candy. Nostrils are round. Tell me this blockage isn't the most amazing thing you've ever seen.

You might say that it was obvious, even way back then, that I was headed for trouble.

~ ~ ~

I'd swarm him as soon as he took off his socks. I found a fresh day's mold irresistible, especially when packaged in new-shoe smell. The most precious substances on earth are matured: Oka cheese, 1983 Chateau Lafite Rothschild, toe funk. I loved watching NBA basketball, because I knew that the players all harbored the same beautiful problem.

His balls were a swamp where I went to get lost: scrotum so rich in folds, trapping his every secretion and distilling it into deliciousness. Piss drops would evaporate there, leaving salty rings that smelled like the semen hidden inside him, a tang like bleach. The scent of his pisshole changed with his diet: tuna, maple syrup, coffee, apples.

Lime Jell-O was a dead giveaway.

Know that I didn't kill myself over a boy. His smells were so much better than he was.

The phone rang during one of our sniff sessions, and I let it go to voice mail. Later, when I checked my messages, I heard my doctor saying she wanted to discuss "some of her findings." I put off calling her back, because it didn't sound like a dermatology issue. It sounded like something I didn't want to hear.

~ ~ ~

This one's a Polaroid. Puberty had finally given me a bit of heft, puffed me out with pride. In the shot, I'm sprouting pubes in both nostrils. With my blackheads and acne, I was engaged in all-out war with the world. My fighting stance was angular and defined, because the sun hit from the side and cast half of me in shadow, like it does with the Great Pyramids at sundown.

You'll have to forgive me for having a superiority complex. It's just that the Egyptians built the pyramids in the shape of noses, and it's all rather flattering…

~ ~ ~

His bike gave me months of pleasure at a time. After a sweaty, summer ride through the city, he'd strip and sink into a chair in front of the TV. A smile would creep across his face as I planted myself between his splayed legs and sniffed his nuts and perineum until I passed out from the concentrated virility. Like breathing pure, scented oxygen. His ass was equally intoxicating.

Pits are nice, but too vanilla. I've always made a point of exploring the uncharted body. The waist and wrist often smell like rubber (underwear elastic, waterproof Casio). Behind the knee can be buttery, and shins can be pine fresh.

We are all synaesthetes but with different wiring. That is to say, our senses are connected in ways we might never understand. For you, the smell of grass burning in the sun will make you feel the snakebite all over again. BBQ chicken will always sound like Radiohead.

For me—a nose—it's the opposite. All stimuli lead to smell, and that's why I'm no longer with you.

One day, the shit hit the fan. This is no cliché, because I could actually smell the feces radiating down as it spun around on the fan blades.

I finally went to see my doctor.

"Chemosensory disturbance," she said.

"What are you talking about."

"You have smell impairment, and it's getting worse."

"Impossible! I could smell you from outside," I said.

"Dysosmia. The smells are distorted. You're already relying on memory, because you're not smelling much."

"You're such a fucking odor-kill. I hate you."

"I'm sorry," she said, "but there are ways to cope with this."

At first, I didn't think it was that bad. The nose is a memory cum-dump; I was a hard drive with forty gigs of RAM that archived every whiff, scent, waft and hint I'd ever detected. I had interpreted this man as a mindmap of smells and could conjure a Smell-O-Vision rendering of him anytime I pleased.

The memories were perfect. But that was exactly the problem. They were sterile.

His hair smelled like Pantene Pro-V, even when he hadn't taken a shower in days, his feet like laundry lint and fabric softener. Crotch? Bicycle seat and Irish Spring soap. My memory had frozen out any trace of raunch. In other words, pure fucking hell.

I was guaranteed a lifetime of smells not worth smelling.

What follows is the text from the back of a box of Lime Jell-O. I hope, for your sake, that you never have to follow these instructions:

Add mix to 1 cup boiling water, stir until dissolved.
Add 2 cups ice-cold water, refrigerate until it sets.
Dive in.

A final photo. I'm sealed in green gelatin, entombed with my too-perfect memories the way pharaohs were buried with their treasures and gems. The Jell-O is in the shape of the Great Pyramid of Giza, replica limestone bricks jagged and crumbling where I jumped in. As limey as lime gets.

What stinks is that when I inhaled for the last time, I couldn't taste a damn thing.

AARON HAMBURGER

Aaron Hamburger was awarded the Rome Prize by the American Academy of Arts and Letters for his short story collection *The View From Stalin's Head,* also nominated for a Violet Quill Award. His next book, a novel titled *Faith for Beginners,* was nominated for a Lambda Literary Award. His writing has appeared in *Poets and Writers, Tin House, Details, The Forward, Boulevard,* and *The Village Voice*. He has received fellowships from the Edward F. Albee Foundation and the Civitella Ranieri Foundation in Umbria, Italy, as well as residencies from Yaddo and Djerassi. Currently he teaches writing at Columbia, NYU, and the Stonecoast MFA Program.

Finders Keepers

Aaron Hamburger

He always knew he wouldn't be able to stay away. And sure enough, he's back, standing behind a table of adult DVD's with his picture and assumed name on the cover. In the picture, he has a full head of hair and a ripped chest. In real life, he wears a rainbow-ringed yarmulke that almost masks his bald spot, a black T-shirt that smoothes out the growing curve of his stomach, as well as denim cut-offs that show off his legs, still his best feature, and a pair of beaten-up construction boots that add an inch to his height. His curls are now flecked with gray on the sides, where they still grow thick. His cheeks and nose have swollen. His jaw line has softened. His arms are melting into flab. And yet his fans still line up for an autographed picture or movie featuring Robbie Hunter, the gay rabbi porn star. Or ex-porn star, to be exact. (Maybe he could have been an ex-rabbi too if he'd gotten past the first year of rabbinical school before dropping out.)

Since quitting the porn business, he has tried beauty school, nursing school, even harbored dreams of law school. He has cleaned houses, served drinks, waited tables, but now, he's finally managed to become his own boss. For the past seven months, he has made his living training dogs. When he can find clients.

His life should not have turned out this way. Okay, he's no Einstein like his boyfriend Jack, but he's no dummy either. In fact, he'd been accepted to fucking rabbinical school (even if it wasn't a top-notch rabbinical school). But the point is, he could have been a professional...something. It wasn't that he'd lacked the smarts, but the discipline.

And now he's stuck manning his own booth at the Gay Erotic Expo, which this month is being held in the French Quarter during the humidity of May in Louisiana. The air outside the air-conditioned hotel where they're having the convention just hangs out, wet and sloppy like the tongue of a St. Bernard. He'd never been to New Orleans before, only knew it by its temptingly sordid reputation, and then those awful news reports during Katrina. So the city's charm surprises him with its gently pretty wrought-iron railings, flickering gas lamps, and the clip-clop of horse-drawn carriages. Walking along, he's tempted to dress up in a top hat and tails and serve tea. The people are very polite. Even the homeless guy who sits on the curb outside his hotel uses elaborately literary metaphors to beg for change. And the other day, while Robbie was eating lunch at an inexpensive restaurant recommended in his guidebook (used, pre-Katrina), a woman at the next table said to him in a lilting accent, "Thank you for visiting our city."

~ ~ ~

To save money, he's staying at the apartment of Christopher Pomfret, one of the convention organizers and a longtime Robbie Hunter fan, who at the airport seemed disappointed to be picking up Ronnie Markowitz of Ridgefield, Connecticut. Ronnie's husband Jack is not happy about the sleeping arrangements, not to mention the trip itself. Not because Jack is a prude (which basically he is) or that he's jealous (which disappointingly he's not), but because he's worried the adoption agency might find out. However, he is letting Ronnie attend because they need the hefty appearance fee and the cash Ronnie will take home with him. They need a lot of money these days, and while Jack's teaching job pays the mortgage and Ronnie's dog training used to be enough for heat and water and cable, their bank account is still far short of what they need for the adoption.

"You should be glad I have something like this to fall back on. At least porn is a recession-proof industry," Ronnie pointed out before he left.

"Oh, Ronnie," Jack sighed, "maybe one of these days you'll get an education and understand what 'recession-proof' really means."

Which Ronnie resents. He's already had plenty of education, maybe not in some idle tower, but in the school of life, damn it. And that's more important than knowing which fork to use at dinner or who won the Battle of Gettysburg, or the answers to all those other questions from Trivial Pursuit, the playing of which accompanied by glasses of white wine is Jack's idea of a fun evening.

"Honey, we're home!" Chris Pomfret had trilled as Ronnie lugged his bags up to the third floor. His apartment, in the heart of the quarter, had a balcony and a black wrought-iron railing that faced the hotel where the convention's taking place, just off Jackson Square. According to Chris, they were on high ground. The place had suffered no damage at all during Katrina.

The interior was absurdly plush and dark, fringed with velvet, trailing draperies and padded with thick Persian carpets. Chris assigned Ronnie to a lacy white daybed that his host had forgotten to clear of its porcelain dolls in hoop skirts and decorative pink-bowed pillows embroidered with flowers.

"First things first," said Chris before Ronnie could unpack and produced a pen and a complete collection of Robbie Hunter's oeuvre, all eleven of his adult films. "We're just mad about you down here."

~ ~ ~

Indeed, Ronnie's table (thoughtfully supplied by Ace in the Hole Productions) is mobbed with Southerners from all corners of Louisiana and its neighbors, places with evocative names like Araby, Chalmette, and Meraux, as well as the further-flung communities of Baton Rouge, Beaumont, Texas, and Hattiesburg, Mississippi. His fans always say where they're from, as if that's supposed to mean something to a Yankee like Ronnie, who only the day before had learned that it was the Mississippi River and not the Missouri that flowed through New Orleans on its way to the Gulf of Mexico.

As the day grinds on, Ronnie wonders what it is about his Jew-shtick that excites these sandy-haired, church-worshipping Southerners with their polite drawls and distressed jeans. He feels guilty accepting their hard-earned cash in exchange for a few seconds of his time, and senses the deflated looks in their eyes as they flash back and forth between his pictures to the real live tubby, balding househusband in their presence. As penance, he skips lunch, but by four o'clock he's starving and scarfs down two overpriced brownies from the hotel espresso bar.

While chewing, he takes out the wallet-sized picture of little Jamal that Jack insists that Ronnie carry with him at all times, to nurture his paternal feelings. Jamal is indeed what might be termed a darling boy with a sweet gap-toothed smile, tight black curls, tufted little ears. Ronnie tries to focus on the picture as Jack has instructed him to do. You are my baby. You are my special prince... Yeah, yeah, yeah, you're a fucking angel, all right? How can he get worked up about a picture, like any number of pictures of five year olds he's seen in the newspaper or at workstations. Jamal is not real yet, and part of Ronnie hopes that he never will be. Maybe some people had been born missing a parental gene.

At the end of the afternoon, Ronnie's pockets are stuffed with even more cash than he'd hoped. That should make Jack happy, he thinks. Exhausted, his face ready to crack from too much smiling and chatter, he staggers across the lobby in a sugar-caffeine daze. All he wants to do is lie down on Chris's daybed with the porcelain dolls, but there's more. He has to attend a Cock-Tail party at a bar on Bourbon Street, and then from there, he trudges over to a catered dinner at the home of one of Chris's friends on a Rue named Dauphine, more drinks at another bar on Bourbon Street. At all of these events, Ronnie does his best to sparkle, regale ogling, moneyed fans with ribald adventures of fucking Max Jason or Aaron Rock or Joey Castro, fill their minds with stories to accompany the images they've already doubtlessly committed to memory from his work.

"Work," they say in a mocking voice, these lawyers, doctors, investment managers in their jeans that pinch but show off what's left of their spreading asses. "Like what you do is work!"

It is work, he wants to tell them. You try putting yourself through vet school while staying up all night with those cameras in your face. (Robbie had tried it and failed, which was why he'd dropped out of vet school.) You try remembering those dumb lines and then saying them with a straight face. You try zipping out of "kinky" costumes and getting a hard-on on cue, then keeping it up, even when you're doing anal and some chocolate leaks out over your dick. You try fucking on a blazing pool deck in summer, getting blisters and heat burns on your ass. You try flirting with a bunch of ignorant educated assholes like yourselves while loaded on vodka tonics. (Ronnie should have been drinking soda, not tonic, because of the calories, but he was working, so he deserved a little treat, right? And he found soda disgusting.)

Finally, they stumble out of the bar into the sultry evening, laughing hysterically for no particular reason. And Chris Pomfret says, "So, Robbie, you feel like bein' naughty tonight?"

These days, the answer to that question is supposed to be no. Jack and Ronnie have been careful to be on their best behavior for years now, in preparation for the magic moment when a judge will declare them to be legal guardians of Jamal. But tonight, perhaps because of something in the free wine at his free dinner, or the free vodka tonics supplied to him at the bar, or the smell of stale beer and powdered piña colada mix that perfumes the air of Bourbon Street, or the sly, suggestive smiles of the fans who'd lined up all afternoon for a chance to press flesh with Robbie Hunter, Ronnie says, "What do you have in mind?"

What Chris has in mind is a bar called Corner Pocket, in the north part of the Quarter, a place that Ronnie's guidebook has warned is dangerous to roam around at night. (However, so much of what is in Ronnie's guidebook no longer seems to be true after Katrina. Reservations are no longer necessary at restaurants. The St. Charles streetcar no longer runs. The men who clear your glasses in the bars are Spanish, not black.) Chris explains that the main point of charm of the Corner Pocket is that local boys go there to dance in their underwear for tips. "They're young, dumb, and cheap. And sometimes cute."

"Give me a minute," says Ronnie. "I just need to make a phone call first."

In Connecticut, where the nights are still cool, thanks in part to a breeze that stirs off their lake, Jack is just finishing dinner with Sylvia and Celia, two of his women friends. One is a white hair stylist while the other is a black stay-at-home mom of twins, but they are interchangeable in Ronnie's mind: fat, single, whiny, superficial, and obsessed with the dating and fashion habits of movie stars, as well as shoes, earrings, and purses that they cannot afford.

"Did you remember what day it is?" Jack says.

No, for the life of him, Ronnie has no fucking idea what day it is.

"Today is Jamal's fifth birthday."

"Oh, yeah, that's right."

"Did you call Ms. Jefferson to make sure she gave him our card…?"

"He's five. He can't fucking read!"

"But she can read. And she can read that we love this little boy and want to give him a decent home. You've been drinking. I'm not going to argue with you."

Ronnie feels very glad to be away until he hears a familiar, plaintive bark. "Is that DJ?" he asks. "He knows it's me calling, doesn't he? He misses me."

"Of course he knows it's you," says Jack, his tone softening. "You can't put anything past that dog. He understands English. I tell him, 'Where's Daddy? Daddy's gone, right? Daddy's in New Orleans, remember?' And he knows!"

Ronnie realizes this is impossible. One of his pet peeves is owners treating their dogs as if they're people. But he loves Jack and DJ and their beautiful home in Connecticut and Jack's wonderful and accepting family who know all about Ronnie's past and find it exotic and interesting instead of shocking and never make jokes or slam down the phone when he calls like Ronnie's mother does, so Ronnie goes along with the charade. "Put DJ on the phone," he tells Jack, so Jack obliges, and for a few seconds, Ronnie hears two loud barks that break his heart.

"I love you," says Jack, and hangs up with a kissing noise.

The sounds of those barks and the kiss makes Ronnie anxious and antsy as they pay their three-dollar cover and enter the narrow bar, where as promised, young, dumb, and cheap young men in underwear dance for dollar bills in front of older, smarter, unattractive middle-aged men. Men like I used to be, Ronnie realizes. When did that "used to" happen? Strange, he never missed it before, always felt grateful for the change and the peace it has brought to his life.

But then he feels a tap on his shoulder, and he turns around to face a slim young man in white bikini underwear, ankle socks, and gym shoes. So lucky, Ronnie thinks, his eyes running up and down the lithe, rippled body of this young man writhing a few inches away. I want to dance naked in public, he thinks, slamming down his drink. I want strangers to grab my fucking cock and yank the fucking thing until it explodes. I want to be a porn star again, not a has-been but a still-is, just for an hour.

The young man licks his index finger, then trails it down Ronnie's chest until he gets to his crotch, which he grabs. "You like?" His skin is the color of brandy, and his hair and eyes are very dark. Is he from India? "I'm Freddy."

"Uh, very nice." Ronnie looks around for Chris, who's already at the bar, waving a sheaf of singles and whooping his approval at a white dancer submitting his crotch to the face of a heavyset black man.

"I'm applyin' to law school," says Freddy, crushing himself against Ronnie's hip. "I just commute down here on weekends for a few bucks. It ain't cheap in law school."

"No, it ain't," says Ronnie, amused to hear himself use the word "ain't" in conversation.

"Where you from?"

"How do you know I'm not from around here?"

"Obvious," says Freddy, turning up his nose. "Everyone from around here's so trashy."

Chris is now enjoying the attention of a diffident young man wearing a baseball cap turned sideways, glossy white track pants, and a fascinatingly monstrous tattoo in gothic letters over his left breast. Ronnie can imagine this guy being an absolute menace in bed. "Excuse me," he says to Freddy. "Who's your friend?"

"I thought you had better taste," Freddy replies. "Catch you later."

Ronnie sidles up to Chris, who's extending a dollar bill toward the tattooed guy's penis. The guy grabs the dollar, then the hand and smacks it on his nipple. Finally he extends his waistband. "Take a look, dude, but don't touch," he says before the waistband snaps back.

"Fuck off," says Chris, walking away. The tattooed guy watches with a smirk.

Ronnie takes Chris's place on the stool. "Buy you a drink?" he says.

"I get all I want for free," says the guy. "Buy one for yourself."

"All right," says Ronnie, orders a vodka tonic, and drinks the whole thing down at once, the way he used to in Manhattan bars, instead of sipping it politely after dinner in front of his fireplace with Jack. They don't have a TV in Connecticut, so they sit there drinking and stare vacantly into the flames. "I'll have another."

"I ain't like these other guys, you know," says the tattooed guy.

"Yeah?" says Ronnie, trying to play it cool.

"Yeah. Some motherfucker tries to mess with me, I don't gotta say nothing." He grins and pumps his fist into his left hand. "I don't say a fucking word."

"I bet you have a big cock," says Ronnie, accepting his second vodka tonic.

"Five bucks, you find out."

"What do I get?" says Ronnie. "A look or a feel?"

"Five bucks you get a nice long look. Ten bucks you get a feel."

"I'll give you a feel for a dollar," says Freddy, coming up behind Ronnie and licking his neck.

"Five bucks says I get a feel," says Ronnie, pushing Freddy away.

"Okay, okay," says the guy. "I treat my customers right." He smirks, a practiced smirk Ronnie knows all too well from some of the amateurs in his old films. Then he turns around, lowers the back of his sweatpants to reveal a jockstrap. "This here's my cash register, dude."

Ronnie takes out his wallet. All he has are singles, so he tickles the young man's ass with them, one by one, then sticks them in the strap of his jock.

"Alright now," says the man, turning around, shifting the waistband down one hip, then the other. "Which hand's getting lucky tonight? Left or right?"

Ronnie extends his right hand, as if to complete a business deal. The young man takes the hand and guides it inside his jockstrap. The penis is thick but resolutely soft. The young man is proud of it. He lets Ronnie tinker in there for fifteen seconds. "Okay, that's enough now," he says. "That's all you get. For five bucks."

"You do anything else for money?" Ronnie asks.

"Naah," says the young man, smirking again.

"Hey, where are you running off to?" Ronnie asks. "Can I buy you a drink?"

"You asked me that already."

"Yeah, I know, I know. Well, look." He takes out a twenty. "Talk to me a while?" he says.

The kid frowns at him suspiciously, then snaps the bill out of his fingers. "Fifteen minutes," he says. "On the clock." He inserts himself between Ronnie's legs and puts his hands on Ronnie's ass and slides his hands up and down. "We have to look intimate, or the boss is gonna make me move on."

Ronnie orders himself another drink. "So, what's your name anyway?"

"Rod Armstrong."

"Rod Armstrong," Ronnie repeats. "Don't you think that's a little obvious?"

"For a while I was Bud Silver. Silver's my favorite color, next to black."

"A-ha."

"But I don't know, Silver sounds kinda Jewy, right? If you want to make it in movies, you need something with more punch to it, you know?"

"I do know. I used to be in the film business myself."

"Yeah, right."

"Honest." He takes out a promotional card from his pocket. While Rod Armstrong looks at it closely, puts it up to his nose, Ronnie finishes his drink. They're going down so smooth tonight. He wonders what kind of vodka they use here, and if he can get it in Connecticut. He holds up a finger. The bartender understands.

"Yeah, the picture looks like you," says Rod Armstrong. "I see it now. Guess you've changed some."

"I guess I have in some ways. But in others, I've still got it."

"Says here your name's Rabbi Robbie? What kind of name is that?"

"My name's Robbie. Rabbi is a title, like priest."

A big smile comes over Rod Armstrong's face. "You're a Jew."

Ronnie nods.

"Well, no wonder you made it in Hollywood." He folds his arms and strikes a defiant pose. "So you think I got a future in movies?"

"I don't know," says Ronnie. "It's going to take me more than fifteen minutes to answer that question." He leans closer to Rod's face as if to examine it like a jeweler with a diamond. "I have to get a good look at you first."

Rod Armstrong slaps Ronnie on the knee. "You're a funny guy."

"You live near here?"

"Me? Hell, no. I'm from New Sarpy."

"Well, I'm staying a few blocks from here, maybe a five-minute walk."

"That so?" Rod Armstrong kisses Ronnie on the forehead. "Time's up, motherfucker."

"I've still got seven minutes."

"May-be," says Rod Armstrong, pronouncing the one word as if it were two, "but your time is up."

~ ~ ~

Ronnie wakes up the next morning on the daybed hugging one of the dolls. His T-shirt is still on, his boots are still on, but his pants and underwear are around his ankles. Flinching in the sunlight that manages to filter through the filmy curtains, he staggers to his feet, pulls up his pants, stumbles to the bathroom, and pulls them down again.

As he comes out of the bathroom, he notices Chris scrambling eggs in the kitchen.

"Hey," says Chris, "you were showing off your assets in your sleep."

It takes Ronnie a minute to slow the pounding in his brain and understand what Chris is talking about. "Oh, oh, yeah. Right."

"Funny, though. It's smaller in real life, when it's off-duty, so to speak."

"I'm a grower, not a shower," says Ronnie, sitting down to his eggs and coffee.

"That's okay. I'm still your number one fan."

"For now," says Ronnie. "But in a few years?"

"Oh, I could never forget Robbie Hunter."

"I wish I could," says Ronnie. "Hey, do I owe you for anything last night? I seem to recall we came back here in a taxi."

"It's on me."

"No, seriously." He feels in his shorts pocket for his wallet, but it's gone.

~ ~ ~

Ronnie imagines New Sarpy as one of those dismal, desolate southern towns from bad TV movies, the kind with lynchings and a dusty general store. But it's actually just a suburb of New Orleans, a few miles past the airport. The owner of the Corner Pocket, a friend of Chris's, volunteered Rod Armstrong's address and real name in exchange for a promise not to press charges.

The house is a modest gray ranch raised on blocks, with a carport out back. Ronnie and Chris park on the street out front, walk up to the front door, and ring. They can hear kids squealing inside.

A tired-looking woman with a dishrag on her shoulder opens the door. Her wiry hair forms a frizzed wreath around her sagging face. "What?" she says.

"We're looking for… your son," says Ronnie.

"I ain't got no son."

"Well, we have this address for…"

"See for yourselves." She flings the door wide open to reveal a living room of girls attacking each other with dented Barbie dolls, and in the middle of them, a young man on his knees trying to fix their dollhouse. The man turns around, and a panicked look crosses his face.

"Sweetheart, you go back to the kitchen," he says. "I got some business with the gentlemen."

"Whatever," she says and shuffles down the hall.

"You both wait outside," says Rod Armstrong, or what remained of him, in a low voice. "I'll be with you in a minute."

He seems smaller inside his house, and his face has a few pimples Ronnie hadn't noticed the night before.

They wait on the patchy lawn, dotted with dandelions and crabgrass. Through the windows, they can hear him yelling, and one of the girls screaming, then crying. And after that, a hard smack and a boom, like a lamp or a table hitting the floor. Then silence. Finally, ten minutes later, Rod Armstrong appears, Ronnie's wallet extended toward them. "You dropped this last night. I was going to leave it at the bar for you, but I forgot."

"I see," says Ronnie, opening the wallet to make sure everything's there and making a mental note to cancel his credit cards when he got home. "It seems a little lighter in the cash department."

"Ronnie, let's go," says Chris.

Rod smirks. "You guys spend more money than you realize when you're drunk."

"Not five hundred dollars worth," says Ronnie.

Rod looks at him a second, looks at Chris, then looks back at Ronnie. "Oh, was that your money? I saw some money laying on the floor next to that wallet, and I thought, now whose is this? Hold on now."

About ten minutes later, he comes back out with four hundred dollars. "I think that's all of it. Or almost all. I did keep a twenty or so, you know, as a kind of reward. Like they say, finders keepers."

Ronnie is about to demand the other hundred dollars, but the front door opens. "Buddy!" screams the woman inside. "Your fucking daughters are waiting for their daddy so they can eat their lunch. And they're whining."

"I told you to stay in the house, bitch! Or are you too stupid to follow a simple direction?"

The door slams shut.

Rod shrugs. "High school sweethearts," he says, then shrugs again and flashes a shy, silly grin. His shoulders are hunched forward, and for that brief moment he looks as young as he did in the bar.

"Come with us," says Ronnie suddenly.

"Yeah, right."

"I'm serious," Ronnie says, touching him on the shoulder. "I can help you. I still know a few people in the business."

"Mister," says Rod, staring at Ronnie's hand with such menace that he jerks it back, "I got a home. I got a family. I suppose you wouldn't know what that's like."

No, I don't, Ronnie thinks with a doomed sigh, but if Jack gets his way, I'm about to. And Jack always gets his way.

"This family of yours, they know what you do on Friday nights?" says Chris.

"They know they got grocery money on Saturday morning," says Rod, straightening his back. "What else they gotta know?"

Neither of them has an answer. Rod goes back into the house and Chris and Ronnie stand on the lawn for a minute watching him go. Then they get into their vehicle and speed back to New Orleans. There's still another day left of the convention.

PAUL LISICKY

Paul Lisicky is the author of *Lawnboy, Famous Builder,* and *The Burning House*. His work has appeared in *Ploughshares, The Iowa Review, Story Quarterly, Lo-Ball, Gulf Coast,* and other magazines and anthologies. He has taught in the writing programs at Cornell University, Rutgers-Newark, and Sarah Lawrence College. He currently teaches at NYU. His collection of short prose pieces, *Unbuilt Projects,* is forthcoming from Four Way Books in 2012.

The Pillory

Paul Lisicky

A replica of a pillory in a replica of a Colonial town. My right arm into the right hole, my left arm into the left. My neck went right through the center. I laughed, not because there was anything remotely funny about being hung up in a cross, but just because it felt good to be away from home, school. The marketplace steamed with activity. The worn patch of grass beside the horseblock, the boxwoods by the cobbler's shop, the flies buzzing above the tidy piles of dung. And it wasn't any wonder that the faces before me receded in the glare. It wasn't any wonder that I stopped thinking of my mother and her neck aches, or my father and his call for constant motion whenever he was home from work, even though we never got anything done. I was giving the wood exactly what it wanted. No one was going anywhere. And it was a relief to admit to what was what.

I didn't think of the other boys once punished like that. I didn't give a thought to the eggs, fruit, mice, and shit thrown at their faces. *There can be no outrage more flagrant*, Hawthorne said, *than to forbid the culprit to hide his face for shame*. But was it shame I felt? I only knew that I was tired of holding myself up. I wanted to cave in and so I caved in. Which was why, after I'd grown used to my new position, I pulled myself out and forgot I had a body.

Or took three steps backward and fell a hard five feet to the ground.

It wasn't me, then, that dropped like a bale of hay from a burning barn. It wasn't me lying on my back as the crowd looked on. Or me, for that matter, covering my crotch with my hand, as if I'd already known that they were hungry for murder.

A little girl screamed, and I was relieved to hear that scream tear through the heat.

Relieved, too, to hear my father walking out of the crowd. Relieved to see the arm he raised, for wasn't that him reaching out to help me up? No, that was the crowd in that arm—I can only see it from here—and he was setting his face for what he didn't want to do, which was to spank me as one spanks an errant child, not a twelve-year-old boy whose voice was on the verge of changing.

Once, twice: who can remember such things? Did I feel it? Did I send myself away? He hit me as the crowd looked on, even as his eyes said, who am I doing this for? Aren't you my son? He stopped and he blinked, as if he hadn't known where he'd gone. Then led me to a tool shed on the periphery, where he cleaned off my knee with a handkerchief he'd pulled from his pocket.

I don't have to say that I spent the rest of the day swimming back and forth across the motel pool until the chlorine stung. I got up. I got up in the way we all get up against the arm that wants to keep us down.

Maybe that's what my father already knew back then. And maybe that's why he brought it up at the dinner table thirty years later, though I'd forgotten it, as I'd forgotten many things by then. His eyes looked through me, past me. He spoke as if that memory were just one more thing he'd been wearing around his neck, and the straight-ahead gaze it required of him was no longer serving him at this late hour, what with the bills stacking up on his desk, my mother in Ranmar Gardens, and the empty rooms of the apartment that needed cleaning.

Which was why I didn't throw the balled-up napkin in my hand, though I'd be lying if I didn't admit to that temptation. I put my hand over my father's. And looked away from the face that didn't need my forgiveness.

D A V I D G E R R O L D

David Gerrold is the author of more than fifty books and hundreds of short stories, essays, articles, and columns. He has written scripts for over a dozen hit television series, including *Star Trek, Twilight Zone, Star Trek Animated, Sliders, Babylon 5, Land Of The Lost*, and *Tales From The Dark Side*. His most famous script is "The Trouble With Tribbles" episode of the original *Star Trek* series. His novels include *When HARLIE Was One, The Man Who Folded Himself, The Voyage Of The Star Wolf, Jumping Off The Planet*, and *The War Against The Chtorr* series. In 1995, David Gerrold won the Hugo, Nebula, and Locus awards for *The Martian Child*, the autobiographical tale of his son's adoption. That story was also the basis for the 2007 movie *Martian Child*, starring John Cusack and Amanda Peet. You can find more information about David Gerrold at gerrold.com.

THIRTEEN O'CLOCK

David Gerrold

thirteen o'clock on a thirsty night, dry and windy after midnight, all the boys have paired up, disappeared into the desert, coupling darkly on the sand, have another beer, there's no place else to go except ride the hog and the hot air roars into your eyes at 70 miles per hour, getting too old for this shit, fucking boring, bored with fucking, bored with chasing fucking, bored with waking up alone, and even more bored waking up with anyone else, and even beer cant cure that, fuck me

except that's the problem, nobody wants to fuck me anymore, too many years, too many beers, and that other thing, the scar that starts above my right eye and crawls down to the corner of my mouth, pulling it down into a permanent scowl, so my face looks like something from a slasher movie, only the scar didnt happen when I was on the bike, but when I got off it, at high speed, using the right side of my head as a brake shoe, which wasnt as much fun as it sounds, not even with three beers

so I gave up on the queerbar for the night, the thing about queerbars, straightmen think you just walk in and get a blow job, everyboy is so fucking thirsty for cock, all you have to do is unzip your dockers, and if it were that easy, I wouldnt be standing in the bar at thirteen o'clock wondering what the hell I'm doing and how I got here and why I dont have any other place to go. So fuckit and before I'm halfway out the door, some guy is asking, hey, isnt that a queerbar, and before I can even turn and look, somebody's swinging something at my head and the old reflexes kick in and I duck sideways and he misses, but then the other guy's got a bike chain, stupid college kid, which I dont mean to grab, but I get it anyway because it skiddles off the cast on my arm before he can swing, indecision maybe, probably his first queer-bashing, blood-simple coward, then I'm holding the chain, one good yank, and he's holding a big handful of me, and his eyes go white just in time as I swing him around and shove him into his boyfriend with the baseball bat, and that's when I see the third one

someone oughta teach these little pricks how to beat up a fag, because they're no good at this at all, the third one crumples up too easily, a backhand across the windpipe, big ugly rings with scratchy things, and he's down, and then I'm back with chainless and bat, shoving chainless into bat and both up against the wall, so bat cant move and chainless is already screaming for mommy, godforbid someone should scar his pretty face like mine

—and something happens—

and that's when I get the idea that all he really needs is to be kissed so I pull him close and cover his scream with the bearded oyster and give him enough tongue to choke a deep throat, and I guess right because just as he's starting to kiss me back, surprising me more than him I think, and if this were a different time and a different place, I bet I could hang his legs over my shoulders, or mine over his, I'm not choosy, except the batboy is screaming and who can concentrate with all that noise

by the time danny-bartender finally makes it out the door with his own baseball bat, I've got two on the ground and one up against the wall with my hand on his throat, the pretty one, and I really do think I could negotiate a relationship out of this, except that even as a "cute meet" this is a little too acute. So I let go of the cute meat, and he staggers forward, almost into my arms, jerks back, looks around, sees the queers piling out of the queerbar and maybe he thinks about running, but before he can send the message to his skechers, it's too late, he's caught

danny-bartender wants to call the police, but I tell him not to bother, because the one guy on the ground is having too much trouble breathing, I didnt think I hit him that hard, but he's got a nasty bubbling cut across his neck, which reminds me of things I saw in the service that I really dont want to think about at all, and the other guy who forgot about holding his bat when holding his stomach and his balls became a lot more important is having his own problems exsanguinating through his nose, so I go and pop open the back doors of my van and toss them in, I sold the hog six months ago and bought the van because it's easier on my bad leg and besides you can sleep in a van if you have to, and someboy asks where are you taking them and even though I want to take them out in the desert and bury them, without bothering to kill them first, I say the emergency room because I've already got enough death on my conscience

prettyboy rides in front with me, the other two moaning in the back, and nobody else wants to come because what queer wants to talk to cops anyway, I'm not worried, nobody fucks with me twice, not when I've got their wallets in my pocket

pull up at the E.R. and I drag them both out the back of the van and through the sliding doors, shouting, "white male, age 20, injury to his trachea, might need to intubate; white male, age 20, needs an X-ray for a cracked rib, broken nose, and someone call the police," and I only have to holler it twice before a doctor and two nurses come running

tell the police I'm emmett grogan, they're too young to know the real emmett grogan, and besides I've got the i.d. that proves I'm emmett grogan, I made it myself, tell the police these two injured boys were just coming out of a gay bar, thirteen o'clock in the night, when they were attacked by queerbashers, lucky for them I was driving my little brother back to campus, I point to prettyboy, and we were just passing by

ex-marine, vietnam vet, ex-corpsman, got the tattoo in san diego, yessir, nossir, I didnt see the attackers clearly, officer, there were four of them, they looked like accountants, or maybe lawyers, probably republicans, you know they like to do that sort of thing, the cops give me the narrow-eyed look and I give them the deadpan, and then the fat one says, well if the victims were coming out of a queerbar they probbly got what they deserved, I dont see any need to pursue this further, and the skinny one adds, but maybe we should notify their parents, they look like college students, and I say, nah, give them a break, they're just kids, maybe this'll teach em to stay away from queerbars

and the fat cop says, nah, once they've been into a queerbar, you cant keep em out, one taste of cock and they're queer for life, so I just look at him deadpan and ask, is sucking cock that good, like he knows, and he blinks for a moment, realizing that he cant answer that question without looking either queer or stupid

back in the van, prettyboy still hasnt said a word, he's scared I'm gonna finish that kiss, or maybe he's hopin, but either way, he's sweating, so I hand him all three wallets, after taking out the cash, my own brand of justice, payment for lesson learned, nearly four hundred total, I drive him to the dorm, and as we pull up, he says, thank you for not reporting me to the cops, and at least he doesnt try to blame the other guys, it's all their fault, it wasnt his idea, he was just tagging along, which is obvious anyway, prettyboy is booksmart, but not much else, at least he knows enough not to say anything that stupid, so I think about all the bullshit I can say back to him and decide not to say any of it, instead I look him straight in the eye and say, the difference between us, someone calls me faggot, they're talking about what makes me happy, someone calls you faggot, they're talking about what makes you unhappy, you figure it out, all that money mommy and daddy are spending to send you away to university, you oughta be smart enough to figure out what you like

and then he does surprise me, he starts to open the door to get out and then he turns back and says, can we talk sometime, and there it is, half past whenever, dry and windy after midnight, and he's got big eyes and chewable lips, and surprise, surprise, my dick can still get hard, so I say yes and how about tomorrow night, and he says pick me up right here, and I'm already thinking, we'll go somewhere out on the other side of the desert where the truth is a lot easier, I know he'll never show up, not after twelve hours of sunlight-thinking, but what the fuck, nobody's waiting for me in the next town either, so why not

sleep away most of the day, crawl out of my coffin just in time to enjoy the sunset, shower and burger at the truck stop, think about beer, but leave it at thinking, not drinking, cruise over to the landing zone and prettyboy is leaning against a wall, he flicks his cigarette sideways, like he thinks that's butch, it isnt, and he strolls over and climbs in the passenger seat and I roll without talking and he doesnt say anything either and I'm wondering what the fuck he thinks is going to happen tonight, because I sure as shit dont have a clue, but this is something better than nothing

we drive for a while, prettyboy finally says something, I was afraid you werent going to come, I tell him I didnt think he'd be there either, so we're even, he asks where we're heading, I shrug and nod ahead; away from the light, because I dont like the light, if it's too bright I can see the scars on my face from the inside, he tells me to stop calling him prettyboy, his name is Michael, I tell him he hasnt earned a name yet, he's still meat, fresh off the plane, and we've got a body bag already waiting with his name on it, deal with it

finally I ask him what the fuck he wants from me, he says he wants to know what I know and I tell him I dont know shit and finally we turn off the highway onto a side road and after a while off the side road onto a couple of forgotten ruts and we go two or three miles up and down bouncing to a place where something used to be, but now there's only hard-packed dirt, and I pull off and turn the engine off and we sit and listen to it cooling in the night

we get out, I go around to the back, pull out a blanket, a couple bottles of water, we sit in the dark, side by side, watching for shooting stars, and except for pointing them out to each other, we dont talk, I'm waiting for him to start, but he doesnt, so after a while, I reach over and grab his hand, not because I particularly want to hold his hand, I dont even fucking know him, but it's a start

he's not good for small talk, neither am I, he asks me how I know how to fight, I tell him the truth, fighting is easier than having the shit kicked out of you, then he asks me about my leg, so I tell him

somewhere in the fucking delta, the hot wind putrid, the whole country stinking like a Saigon whorehouse, disintegrating with the smell of shit and incense and rotting vegetation, all mixed with the spices they use to hide the fact that the meat is rotten before they even get it into the pan, even if you knew what it was—dog or cat or rat—who the fuck cares, when you get hungry enough, you stop asking questions

they call it a road, but it's just a lousy stinking dirt scar, a slash of mud carved between two fields, the crapgrass rippling in the wind—the distant edges bordered by trees, a fucking perfect place to die, a fucking bullseye for an ambush—the lieutenant holds up a hand and we all stop, then he holds his arm straight out and waves us down—and we scatter into the grass and disappear

they say that charlie is terrified of us, because we're monsters, bigger and healthier and better fed, better guns, better ammo, better supplies—and better targets too—those little human cockroaches scuttle down into the ground and disappear, trapdoors in the floor of the world—everybody knows they're all underground, the delta is tunneled from here to forever, underground cities, you could walk all the way to uncle ho without ever seeing daylight—and maybe they're right, maybe the little fuckers are scared shitless, but I dont think so

claymore—we call him that because he's good at taking mines apart—he grins and whispers across to me, it's a good day to die. I tell him to shut the fuck up. it's never a good day to die, but he saw that in a movie and he thinks it's cool—it isnt cool, it's fucking stupid—and what are we waiting for anyway?

the lieutenant is yabbering into the field phone, the sweat is rolling down the inside of my shirt, the sun is a hundred and thirty degrees and we're all carrying fifty pounds of field gear—whose good idea was this anyway?—the field isnt a field, it's a fucking swamp, we're up to here in mud so deep that every step, the mud is fighting to pull my boots off—and I cant stand too long in one place, I start to sink deeper

oh man, I am going to stand for an hour in the shower tonight and I dont fucking care what color the water is

the lieutenant he stands up and waves us back to the road—whatever—he does this five, six times an hour—squelching up out of the mud, and before I can yank my boot free, the world fucking blows up in my face—all the different colors of orange and white and red and black, all at once, and everybody's screaming because the shit is going off all around us—they're dropping fucking mortar shells on us, and they've got our range because the crap is hitting left and right and up and down—claymore flies apart in pieces, a fucking good day to die my fucking ass—and I'm too busy pulling my goddamn leg out of the mud to be scared—we're all firing wildly at the distant trees, like we're really going to hit something, we're fucking dead out here

rocks and shit and mud comes pattering down, all around, a pummeling of earth, it goes on forever while the ground shakes and your ears bleed and the world turns sideways and knocks you assover everywhere, and no my leg isnt supposed to bend like that, but I cant feel it anyway, and I cant find my fucking gun and while my hand is flailing around everything turns orange, the sky, the muck, a wall of heat knocks me flat into the shit, rolls me sideways, and then I hear the first roar of the flames—a roiling carpet, napalm forest, blossoming scars across the whole west side of the world, and for a moment, there's a kind of peace, the explosions stop, shocked in fucking horror, roasted alive, who fucking cares, I fade out and over, something is whupping up and I feel nothing

while I'm dead everything is fine, because I cant feel anything, I dont care, I could go on like this forever, white light and voices

—something happened—

but then it's gone, leaving only a memory of a memory, a sense that there was something *important,* maybe it was the drugs, but no, I know drugs and this wasnt drugs, this was something *else,* but it's gone, it's like hearing the echo, but not knowing what clanged, the feeling stays with me all the way across the pacific and down into the crevices of San Francisco, it never fades, a sense of muffled awareness, the doctors tell me it's resonance, it'll go away, but they're wrong, it doesnt—never completely, it just drifts behind-inside forever, it doesn't bother me, it just turns into something to live with, like the plastic leg

so I spend a few years riding a hog up and down the left coast, cruising up through Big Sur, across the big red bridge, up through Marin, into the cold wet wild north where the trees make green canyons, up into Oregon where the green is too thick and I start thinking about Charlie creeping through the green, if Charlie had green like this, we'd still be there, it's nothing like the Delta, first of all the smell is sweet and green and wet, but I cant shake the feeling that something is creeping up after me, so I keep riding, on up as far as Puget where the only difference between the fog and the rain is that the fog is thicker and wetter and from there up to the border where the Canadian customs guard is so exquisitely polite I know he hates to let me in, but he cant find a reason not to, I'm legal, I just look ugly, so on into Canada, eh, all the way up to Alaska and I lose myself for a few years with the bears and the salmon and the air so crisp it cuts like ice through the tent, through the sleeping bag, and man I'm getting too old for this shit, but I gotta know what it was, and for some reason I've made up my mind that the Inuit know, some shaman or medicine man, whatever, because maybe underneath, there's some magic here

and maybe there is, but I never find it, so I come sliding back south, dropping down through Idaho, following the Snake river all the way down, passing through forgotten dusty places with names too small for the map, endless dry highways, into Nevada with its desolate empty stretches of baking summer east to Utah where the canyons still echo with fossilized time, south to New Mexico with its hidden villages carved into orange sunset cliffs, west to Arizona and up the poisonous side of Superstitious Mountain, maybe there's a wise old grandfather, the Hopi know life out of balance, and eventually south through Mexico, where I spend a week or a year or whatever living the way of the whaqui, eating mushrooms and peyote and rattlesnakes, fucking everything that I can push down on its back or its stomach, if it's a hole and I'm horny, I dont care anymore, it doesnt matter, there's that instant of orgasm, that quick throb-and-spurt of time where I stop existing long enough that the nagging sense of something unsaid and left undone is pushed so far out of my consciousness that it almost doesnt exist for that moment, and the lassitude afterward, on my back and staring dispassionately at the glowering sky, waiting for wisdom and insight, that connection of time and place and understanding, but all I accomplish is a thousand light-year stare with nothing on the other side, and one day I put the hog back together, get the engine running, tune it, tweak it, test it, over and over, until it sounds like magic growling again, until one day it's right, and the moment is right, and I get on and start riding, just a test ride, I say, but I keep riding north and never look back, I run out of gas at a queer hippie commune south of Tuscon and live in a teepee while I flush out all the crap from my system, lose twenty pounds of Mexican bad shit and end up with abs again, stumping up and down the rows of corn and beans and tomatoes, digging latrines, carrying water, hoeing and weeding, learning to serve others again, and for the first time in longer than I can remember actually earning the right to feel good about myself at the end of the day

but its all queerboys here and I'm not ready to give up girlpussy forever, it's fixed in my mind now that there's boypussy and girlpussy, and each is fine in its own way, and by now I've even learned there's other things to do and maybe that's part of the answer, if not *the* answer, it's still part of it, because what these queerboys have learned is that it's not about fucking, it's about people, a strange place to learn this

and then, in an angry flash, I dont know how it happens, I'm back on the left again, Arizona a red and gold memory in the rear-view mirror, how did that happen?—the moving finger writes and once it writes you're fingered, I come bouncing down into the Castro where I hook up with Bloody Mary, a bulldyke who rides a hog and sometimes she rides me and sometimes she rides the hog and once she rides us both at the same time and I ask her how can she be a dyke if she's riding the rod and she just laughs and says it isnt about pussy, it's about people, so I'm not the only one who's figured that out

we coast up to Guerneville where nobody cares, where we're out of earshot of the creepazoids who think we're traitors to the fag-flag because we're bumping each other ugly, except one night I break my leg in Sausalito, laying down the bike to avoid a drunken spoiled teenage bitch, and if I could have gotten up afterward I'd have punched her a new one, but I cant get up because the bike is on top of me, she jumps out and starts wailing about the dent I just put in the side of her new car that daddy just bought her only two days ago for her seventeenth birthday, while I'm still lying under a bleeding hog and

—it happens again—

until Mary the dyke slaps her, takes away her new expensive toy, this thing called a cell phone, and punches 911 and calls an ambulance, and I'm off to the E.R. tonight and the V.A. tomorrow, and fortunately it's the plastic leg that's broken and six weeks later, the V.A. finally puts me on a new one, a better one, and I'm ready to get back in the saddle, except

I dont want to, something's happened; I cant explain it, but something's happened, and even though I feel like a cowboy who has to shoot his horse, I sell the hog, what's left of it, and no, it isnt fear, I could get back on the bike in half a minute, I trust myself on the road, I dont trust anyone else, I trust my ability to keep out of their way, but if a seventeen-year-old bitch can put me down in the gutter, maybe it's the universe sending me a message; the dyke tells me I'm a pussy, so I know she doesnt understand, and fuckit, I'm not even sure I understand it myself, all I know is it's time to let go, the bike isnt me anymore, and neither is the dyke

and then time flashes and I'm living out of the back of a VW bus, I dont even remember where I got it, but the feeling is there, I can drive out to the middle of the Mojave, get off the highway, get off the side road, find a dirt slash into the middle of nowhere, someplace even the lights in the distance are too far away to look like anything more than stars glimmering through the bottom of the world, and I lay down on my back and look up at the diamond sky and it's like riding the hog again, only this time riding it through time and space, I'm standing at the front of starship earth and sailing forward like I'm king of the universe and I can hear the feeling loud and clear like picking up clear channel KOMA from five states away and I know it's not the tequila and it's not the grass and it's not a fucking acid flashback either, it's something else, and I can feel the throb and pulse of the ground beneath my body and I know the ground doesnt throb and pulse, so what the flaming fuck am I feeling, it's just my own heartbeef, slabs of muscle too stubborn to stop slamming the blood through my veins, and what the fuck is life all about anyway, but the feeling, it wont go away, it's like music sometimes, a distant chorus, very faint and far away, under the edge of the horizon, like those things whatever they are that always woke me when I was little, going *hoo-hooo* in the night

and I tell prettyboy, that's what I know, that I'm just another hood ornament on the battering ram, wherever it goes, I get there first, hardest—I'm the part that takes the impact—but every time, just before the collision, I get this flash, like there's something under the bottom of the world, calling to me, I dont know what the fuck it is, but I cant get away from it, cant get it to shut up, cant forget it, and cant fucking die until I find out what it is

so now it's his turn to explain and he tells me there's nothing to explain, he isnt anybody at all, he doesnt, just doesnt, and it doesnt matter that there's no predicate to that subject, I get it because I've been there, I'm still there, I live there, we all do, only some of us know it

he says it started in bed, in bed with a girl, she was warm and round and luscious like something out of a painting by Rubens or maybe Titian and he just wanted to float on top of her like she was a giant delicious waterbed, he wanted to suckle at her breasts and bury his face in her juicy cunt and it surprised him when I said, yeah, I know, except whatever else she was, she wasnt either, and she wouldnt

they'd lie together, spooned, his arm curled around her side, but once when his fingers start tentatively brushing at her thigh, she mumbles not now, and another time when he brushes at her lips, the lower ones, probing for her clit, she pushes his hand away roughly as if he's an intruder, and still another time when he moves his fingers up to circle her great pancake-sized nipples, she rolls away, is that all you ever think about, so he turns on his side and tries to sleep while this great moby of desirability rests naked behind him, his cock still stiff, his balls aching, and the next morning as he's pulling his tighty-whites up and over the tentpole, she sits up in bed and complains that he's unromantic, that he doesnt want to do it with her, and it's because she's fat, isnt it, and to his credit he doesnt say anything, he just finishes pulling up his pants, he buttons his shirt and slips into his sneakers and closes the door behind him, all without a word or even a look, because inside he's feeling so—there isnt really a word for that feeling, but that's what he's feeling, so he leaves and three nights later he's outside a queerbar with two guys he barely knows, it doesnt make sense, but nothing in life makes sense, why would anyone want to fuck a guy when there are all these beautiful fat women around, except if they dont want to fuck, what's a guy to do, get desperate, and he's almost ready to cry, except he's still too full of that other feeling

so there we are, I have too much life and he doesnt have any, so I hold his hand and after a while he leans up against me, and we sit there listening, he listens for what I can hear and I listen for silence

are you going to fuck me, he asks, and I dont answer for a while because I dont know the answer, I dont know if I want to fuck him, he's pretty enough and after that kiss, I didnt figure it would be that hard to get his ankles behind his neck, or mine, it doesnt matter, but I dont know if it's worth the effort, fucking for the sake of fucking sounds fine when you're fifteen, but not when the digits are reversed, so I'm sitting there wondering why he asked, is it something he wants or is it something he's afraid I'm going to do to him whether he wants it or not, and just the fact he asked the question scares the shit out of me, not the scared-shitless feeling like when live fire is making a three-foot ceiling over your head, but the other-scared feeling of just not knowing who you are or what you're supposed to do, a feeling I thought I'd left behind in Alaska or Mexico, or maybe certainly in Arizona, or probably somewhere since then, but finally I just say, is that what you want and he doesnt answer, because I figure he's probably sorting it out the same way

then the moment passes, and I know we're not going to fuck, not then, and probably not ever, but I've been wrong about that before, so we both just relax, now that the question's been asked, not answered, but resolved anyway for the moment, and I'm sitting there thinking a whole fucking epic, and he says, thank you, and I ask, for what, and he says, for listening

and yeah, I get it, and I say so, and he asks, does this feeling ever go away, and even though I'm not sure what feeling he's talking about I still know the answer, I shake my head, I say no, it never does, you just learn to live with it; he breaks away, he sits opposite so he can look at me, the moon is up now, half-past full, so there's enough light I can see his eyes are bright, and yeah, he's getting prettier by the moment, and I'm almost rethinking the answer to his question, but I'm not, because it still isnt happening and in the moonlight, I know why

there's this guy I knew once, his name was Jerry, we went to the same high school, we never talked to each other, we just saw each other in the hallway sometimes, and sometimes at the Big Boy where he was bussing tables, working his way through community college, but we werent in any of the same classes there either, we just saw each other around, and then I forgot about him, the way you forget most of the people you bump up against as you stumble along, until one night a few years later, it's the collapsing end of 1969, and I'm in a boy-bar on Santa Monica Boulevard, and I see him sitting alone in the corner in the back patio and he looks like Wiley Coyote right after the rocket exploded in his face, so I go over and say hi, and he says hi back and I ask him what's wrong, and he cant even get it out, he just looks at me with a look I've only seen one other time, a year later, in the Delta, when Perry the black kid with the big round eyes caught one and just looks at me, his hands across his belly, all his dark red blood pulsing out between his fingers, trying to push his guts back in, and he looks at me, our eyes meet for just a second, and the expression on his face says it all, please tell me I'm going to be all right, tell me I'm not going to die, and he knows I wont lie to him, and I lie and say, hey man, just hold on, just hold on, and the medic stings him with morphine and his eyes stay fixed on mine the whole time, and then the blood stops pulsing and he's dead, but his eyes are still wide, and that's the look that I saw on Jerry's face, like he was asking me to tell him that he wasnt dead yet

but that hadnt happened yet, this was the first time I ever saw this look, and it stopped me cold, because I didnt know a human face could look like that, and it froze me—the terror, the desperate need, I thought I should do something, except I wasnt in that bar to be Mary Poppins, I was looking for some boypussy, and I was this close to saying, fuckit, tell it to the chaplain, tell it to someone who cares, someone who's paid to care—but then he says, tell me why I shouldnt kill myself and I didnt have the sense to back away quickly, so I stand over him, instinctively shielding him from the light and the noise and the stink of cigarettes and beer and Old Spice and I listen—and what he tells me, well, it almost saves my life

see, he wasnt making it, it was the end of the fucking sixties for god sake, everything was falling apart in slow motion, and all anybody could do was get stoned and fuck their brains out, so that's what we did, all night long, every night, there wasnt any daytime anymore, just the long long night of parties—only Jerry was alone, one of those guys who never quite finds the rhythm of anything, he didnt know how to be whatever it was he was supposed to be, nobody did, and everybody's walking around saying stupid shit like, "hey man, where's it happening?" and you have no fucking idea how dumb that sounds, it's like admitting you're so lost you cant even see the party even when it's happening around you, it was happening everywhere and it wasnt happening anywhere, because whatever was happening, it was only happening when you made it happen, but most of us never learned that lesson, or died trying, so even though Jerry didnt understand it, that was the thing that made him just like everybody else because nobody understood it yet, but Jerry was one of the smart ones, so smart he was stupid; he thought the world was gettable, and because he thought that, he thought that there were people who actually did get it, in fact Jerry thought that everybody did, probably already had, except they'd all privately agreed not to let him in on it, none of it made sense and nobody was letting him in on the joke, so after a while he gives up, just gives up completely and resigns, stops waiting for Santa Claus and starts waiting for rigor mortis, he's ready to be just another one of those used-up boys propped up against the bar like scenery—the ones who've been entered too many times and finally abandoned all hope, the ones who settle for fucking as a substitute for loving, nowhere near a fair trade, but if you fuck long enough and hard enough, sometimes you dont notice, trust me on this

except fucking-God's a practical joker, because just when Jerry decides there aint no such thing as either God or love, that's the afternoon, God drops a beautiful redheaded boy on him, and the two of them do something right and instead of just falling lustfully into bed, mindlessly fucking their brains out on each other's flesh until half-past seeyaround, instead it's too hot to fuck, so they sit and talk for five hours on this sweaty July afternoon, and instead of thinking only about their dicks, they actually work a little higher up, the other end of the spinal cord, and not until the day finally cools off do they end up in bed, but that's only because it's a more comfortable place to just strip down to your jockeys and relax, surrender to the moment, because it doesn't matter anymore, you dont have to pretend now, just be who you are, and they still dont fuck, they share a big glass of ice water and keep talking, and it doesnt matter what they're talking about, they're just having this amazing adventure talking and discovering, and even after they get naked—and you know how you get naked in front of other guys, there's this thing, you know the thing, where you really dont want them looking at you, because you know they're sizing you up, judging how good you look or how big you are, and you know you're never going to look as good as the guys in the magazines, and you end up feeling that you dont want to be naked in front of anyone because you dont want them thinking you're not good enough—except that doesnt happen here, they end up sitting together naked, unashamed, each one astonished at how beautiful the other one is, and they still dont fuck, they hug and kiss and touch in wonder, and they laugh a lot at some shared joke of intimacy, and finally take a shower together and laugh a whole lot more, and then they hump and bump a little, even a lot, but they keep interrupting themselves to talk and to share, and before either one of them has come anywhere near to that moment where it's time to get a towel and wipe off and make a hasty graceless exit, they realize that—*something is happening*—it's silly, so fucking silly, because there's no such thing as love at first sight, it's just a fairy tale, but there they are anyway, falling ass-over-teakettle, tumbling over the cliff of joyous delirium, so full of happy giggling exuberance it doesnt make sense, until Jerry has impossible tears running down his cheeks and he wants to run out in the middle of the street and yell to the whole world, dont you dumbfucks get it, love—*real love*—really is possible, and if Hitler had ever had sex this good, World War II would never have happened, that's what it feels like, fucking so good you feel sorry for Hitler, and he and the redheaded boy roll together, laughing

but look, it isnt about the sex at all, it was never about the sex, everybody thinks it's about the cocks and the cunts and the mouths and the assholes, all that juicy pistoning, the hot wet pumping in-and-out, but it isnt, it's about the thing that happens *during* sex, if it's right, if everything is right between the two people, whoever, whatever, if there's a real connection, then the sex is just a way to get even more connected, because it's the connection you want, not the sex—because the truth is, when you're fucking, it's not about you, it's about the person you're with, because if it isnt, then you're the biggest dumbfuck of all, just licking the menu instead of eating the meal—and that's the magic that Jerry and his beautiful redheaded boy fell into

yeah, I know, it doesnt make sense to sit and talk with someone from four o'clock in the afternoon until nine in the fucking ayem the next morning, when you have to get up and go back to work, and on the basis of that short time know that this is the person you want to spend the rest of your life with, that all you want from existence is to keep on exploring the landscape of this beautiful incredible godling, discovering yourself in his smile and his laughter and his cockness, but it happened to them, both of them, they connected anyway, and in the days after that first incredible revelation of each other, it just gets better, they start learning how to do all the other things that people do when they fit their lives together—they talk to each other on the phone every day for three weeks, grabbing every moment they can between their respective jobs and obligations and it should have been perfect, because each of them was exactly what the other one wanted and needed, they fit, you know, they just fit, and every moment was well, you know, just perfect

and then it all comes apart, because Jerry makes a stupid mistake, the biggest stupidest mistake anyone can make, he gets scared, he stops trusting his instincts, because see, the redheaded boy wants to get serious, I mean serious with a capital lets-move-in-together, and Jerry panics, because he thinks it's getting too intense, he cant deal with it, he doesnt know how—I mean, how do you explain it to mom, right?—because nobody gives lessons to queerboys how to have a real relationship, and make it work in a world that mindlessly believes that this thing that brings you so much joy is so despicable that God hates you for it, and the whole thing scares him, so instead of being home, he leaves a note on the door and goes out cruising instead, not because he wants to cruise, but because he doesnt know what else to do, but he's so fucking confused, so the redheaded boy takes the note off the door and goes out looking for something else to do and he picks up a hitchhiker, no, not quite, that's not where this story is going, let me finish, and the hitchhiker is caretaker at some estate up in Benedict Canyon, so the redheaded boy drives him up there and they talk for a while, but they dont really connect, so after a while, the redheaded boy picks up the phone and calls Jerry, and Jerry is back home by now—see, here's what happened, Jerry cruises and cruises and realizes that cruising is empty, because now that he knows that there's something else, cruising is meaningless, and now that he knows what the something else is, he knows what a jerk he's been for leaving that note, for not being home, and all he really wants to do tonight is curl up with his beautiful redheaded lover and not have to talk, just be in his arms and never be apart again, he's ready to jump off the diving board and say yes, I will

only on the way down the hill, the redheaded boy runs into some drug-crazed hippies, and they shoot him in the face, and then they go into the house and murder four other people, five if you count the unborn baby, and Jerry stays up all night wondering where his lover is, and he doesnt find out what happened until he opens the newspaper Sunday morning, still with me, and he goes crazy, and I dont mean crazy like banging into the walls, raging with grief, I mean crazy like you dont know, nobody knows, because they dont know how to show it in the movies yet, I mean crazy like staring into space crazy, zombie-crazy, desperate crazy, and who the fuck can he talk to about it, because who in the world would understand, certainly no straight man, maybe another faggot, except all he knows about boy-bar faggots is that he doesn't trust any of them either, he knows who they are because he's one of them too

and it's two-three months later, and the murderers still havent been caught, and he tells me all of this in the back patio of a sleazy boy-bar in West Hollywood because he has no other place to go, and of all the places to go, this is the worst, because it just puts him back where he was before, but he cant be what he was before, because this time, now, he knows what he doesnt have, and that's when the tears start running down his cheeks, all he had was three weeks, hardly enough time to make any memories at all, just a couple of fucks and a drive around the city, and all he can think of is that he's never going to see his lover again, the most precious person in his life, never again, and all the memories they're never going to have, all the pillow conversations, and why the hell should he keep on living if the best part of his life is over

but see, here's how I know that God is a malignant thug, a practical joker, an asshole—if he wouldnt listen to his own son's prayers on the cross, why the fuck do you think he's going to listen to anyone else's?—here's the joke, Jerry looks at me like I'm supposed to say the one thing, whatever it is, that makes a difference, except I dont know what the fuck it is, how the hell should I know how to save his life, because I cant even save my own, because I've got my goddamned draft notice in my back pocket and I have to report the day after Thanksgiving, and in three-four months, just in time for the rains, I'll be slogging through the goddamn Delta with all the other dead men walking, and I'm thinking what the fuck, maybe I should run for Canada instead, I can be there in a straight two day run, or maybe I should just tell them I like sucking cock and fucking ass, at least that's honest, except I'm not ready to be that honest yet, nobody is, except I also heard that they dont even care anymore, the draft boards, they just have to generate so many bodies a week, fill up the green uniforms, fill up the body bags, and this week it's me and next week it's you, it's all the same, and Jerry looks up at me and says, so okay, now you tell me—why shouldnt I kill myself?

I dunno, why shouldnt he? He's made a pretty damn good case, except forever is a long time, and I'm thinking if I were a sky-pilot, I'd know the right thing to say, except I'm not, and I dont, and besides, if I said the crap they say, we'd both know it's crap, so I say what's in my head, and I say, I am so fucking jealous of you I can't believe it, and his eyes go wide, and I just keep talking anyway, because man, you found it, even if it was only for three weeks, you had it, man—I never did, and you know something most of the rest of us can only wish for, and he looks at me, not getting it, and I dont know where the words are coming from, I just blurt it out—real love, man, you had it, someone really loved you, the rest of us we're standing around and pretending that we're not standing around and pretending, but you—man, you're lucky everybody else in here doesnt beat you to death out of sheer fucking jealousy, because what you had, you had the *real*, not the pretend, You. Had. *It.*

and maybe that was what he needed to hear, and maybe what he said was what I needed to hear—that it really was possible, because up until then, I didnt know it, maybe nobody did, Jerry was the first person I ever knew who found love, the first one who could actually say it, and while he's crying for what he's lost, I'm wishing I were him, I want what he had, even if it's only for three weeks or three days or three hours

and as I'm telling all this, as it's all pouring out of me in one dumb rush, I look across at the prettyboy and see only blankness in the eyes and I realize he doesnt know what I'm talking about, cant know, because he's never done it, never been there, never had that rush of endorphins, that wave of physical amazement that starts in the bottom of your dick and comes tidal-waving up your spine like some kind of astonishing hot tsunami and floods up inside of you, inside your heart, your whole chest, chokes up your throat, and floods your eyes with tears of wonder and joy, he's never known it, that's the fucking tragedy, he's never been there and the question of sex with him, of fucking him, it's finally answered for me, because if there's no connection, then all it is, it's just fucking exercise, and I've had enough exercise for ten lifetimes—I dont want to wake up with an intimate stranger, someone who knows the taste of my sweat, but not the taste of me, just another zombie-fuck

but there was that moment, I know it happened, when he *kissed back* and something flickered in that moment and that's the moment I'm speaking to—who was that?—and how do I get back there, how does anyone

did he kill himself, prettyboy asks, it's the wrong question, I shake my head, to tell the truth I dont know, I never saw him again, maybe he did, maybe he didnt, maybe he just stumbled out into the night, just like everybody else, you crawl into your coffin and dont come back out until it's time to feed again

I stand, stretch, listen to the bones tap-dancing against each other, stretch again, denying entropy one more time, start picking up blankets and water bottles, is that it, he asks, and I turn and look at him, what did you want, and he doesnt answer, doesnt have an answer, and maybe that's the greater tragedy, worse than knowing what you want and never having it is never knowing, never being able to speak it at all

headed back in silence, bumping over the hard-packed dirt, finally up and onto the asphalt again, sliding through the dark, the wind roaring like a jet engine, and still he doesnt talk, for some reason he doesnt look so pretty anymore, and I'm wondering why I bothered, why I wasted my time, and why I didnt fuck him anyway, except even an old boar like me has some pride

—something happened—

I never talk about the *blinks*, nobody understands, I tried a couple times, but I got the look, that look, the one that says I'm going to pretend I understand you, but only for as long as it takes to gnaw off my leg and escape, and no we cant ever be drinking buddies again because you're crazier than me, there's something scary-wrong in your head, so I learned the hard way, I just dont talk about the *blinks*, not to anyone, and when they happen, they happen, nobody around me notices, so maybe I am crazy, it's like somebody cutting into the movie, just a dazzling flash of bright, way too fast to see, you only realize it afterward, except afterward there's the burn-in still hanging in the air, the after-images of whatever seared into my existential retinas never found anybody who knew about it, even with careful asking, none of the gurus, nor the medicine men, the shamans, not the dopers and dealers neither, asked a few doctors and corpsmen if they'd ever heard of anything like it, but they just looked at me funny, so I dropt the subject

only once, the crazy dyke, late one night on the road, somewhere between nowhere and nothing, we finally pull over and fall out onto our blankets, eventually end up on our backs, first her, then me, then both of us, staring up at the stars—*something happens*—and I ask her, did you feel that, and she asks, feel what, and I try to explain, and she says, you got *pinged*, and I say, pinged, what's that, and she says, it's when somebody is checking you out, seeing if you're there, like submarines in the dark, and she says no, it's like computers on a network, I *ping* you and you *pong* back, except you aint ponging, but someone's definitely pinging

and that's as far as that conversation goes, but it sticks, enough so that whenever—*something happens*—I'm listening to hear who it is, or *what*, aliens or angels or Ida Noh, the mystery whore of Saigon, how'd you get the clap, soldier, Ida Noh, sir—I'm listening, listening like the antenna at Arecibo

except I'm always listening *after*, never during, never before, it's like lightning, you only know you've been struck by it when you pick yourself up off the ground afterward, like Jerry and his redhead, and I figure that maybe I'm the wrong kind of receiver, or maybe I'm not getting the whole signal, or maybe I'm in the fringe area, Ida Noh again, and the only part of any of it that I can be sure of is that it never happens when I'm alone, it only happens when I'm with someone and only when the moment is intense, very intense, too intense, almost overload, that's when it happens, when the meter is pinned

other people, they talk about those moments when everything happens at once, when the car starts to skid, when it goes skidding/swerving/screeching/sideways, that's the moment when time stops for them, for me that's the moment when time disappears, and I come out the other side still ringing all over, reconnecting to myself, I know I'm missing something here, I used to think that if I could find someone else, anyone who experienced the same thing, then maybe we could, Ida Noh, connect, and if it happened to us together, at the same time, maybe we could get a clearer signal, except when I talk about the blinks, the pings, I get the stare, the what-are-you-talking-about look, so that's not an option except yeah, at the back of my mind, I'm still always thinking, maybe this one, maybe this time, maybe finally I'll find out who's calling, who's pinging, and sometimes I'll go days/weeks/months without a ping and I'll miss it for a while and then I'll get used to the silence and then I'll even forget about the pings for a while, until it starts again, and once, lying awake in some strange bed in the middle of some strange night, I had this thought that maybe I'm only one piece of the circuit, like a transistor or a capacitor or one of those other bits of electric magic, and maybe what I need isnt another piece like me, but some other piece totally unlike me, maybe I'm just an antenna, maybe I need a modulator or a resonator or maybe just a tuning knob, maybe there's a whole bunch of pieces missing, and maybe I'm not anything at all, just a chimpanzee hammering on a rock and striking the occasional spark

that's the other thought, that whatever it is, maybe it's something I cant know, maybe none of us can, because we're not there yet, we can string some wires and make electricity run around in circles and sparkle some lights, but we still cant do that next thing, whatever it is, that next thing that comes after super-sharp televisions and super-fast computers, that thing that we still havent thought of, whatever it will be, and by comparison with that, we're still just apes with bones and flints, and that's the thing I think about listening to the stars, listening for others, maybe we're listening with the wrong ears, and we cant really hear whoever is pinging, maybe only a few of us can hear occasional bits and pieces of the pings and the rest of us cant hear anything at all because we're just not there yet, we're still in bed with Ida Noh in the hot damp nights of Saigon

and oh shit, Saigon, and Perry, late one night, we play cut-for-low and loser takes the point next day on patrol, and it's Perry who catches it in the belly, not me, and it's Jerry all over again, only this time it's me with the guilt, with the story, it's my fault he died, I only lose a leg, but Perry spills his guts, and ever since then I've been spilling mine, only I never get to die, Perry was the lucky one, he got out quick

and I get it, I get it *again*, we're all dragging dead bodies around, offering each other a sniff of the corpse, the past is this heavy ruck that sits on our backs, growing heavier every year, we just keep adding more and more shit to the load, and eventually history is inescapable, the shitbird guru on my shoulder yabbers into my ear, the past defines not just the present, but the future as well, there's no escape, is there, this is it, and that's why I didnt fuck the prettyboy, because there's no place in my past for that future

finally bring him back to where we started, the big empty parking lot below the dorm, pull to a stop, we look at each other, all the stuff still unsaid, the real stuff that nobody ever says, and just before the seeya—*something happens*—and the van starts shaking, hard, like something slamming against it from the side, again and again, and then the lights of the world come on, dazzling, finger-stabbing, searching, finally pinning us in the van, and there's a great whooshing noise and screaming too, all the voices in the world, prettyboy grabs my hand and

—it happens—

He's turned pretty again. Pretty frightened. Everything slows down, stops. The eye of the timestorm. Even while the banging continues around us.

—connection—

all the flickers, all the blinks, everything, time and space collapses into one moment, and this time I'm in the moment, caught, a dragonfly in amber, gossamer wings transparent in the heavenly backlight, and in the same instant, everything simultaneous

—I get it—

There's Jerry and Perry and Mary the bulldyke and even prettyboy, and all the rest of us, everyone who connected, who flickered in and out, all of us woven like ganglia into the great neural web of sentience recognizing itself. That's who's been pinging—not aliens or angels or anything else—*it's us*. All of us together. That's the connection. Our own humanity is calling. It's the next step. It isnt a secret, it never was, except all of us together, we never knew, or we keep forgetting, or we do it on purpose, but now this time—*some of us* can actually see it happening—

—the fireflower blossoms—

A hot rush, a tidal wave, tsunami of exuberance, rising up through me, I can see to the end of the universe and back, all of us, connecting, lighting up, answering the pings, awakening to ourselves, blinking alive, confused, excited, wondrous, not everyone yet, but all of us who've heard the wake-up call, and in that moment, we're together, and we *know*, and it's *now*, and there's *no* going back

—Oh—

and then as the van topples and crashes sideways onto the street, the sirens come whooping in, the red and blue lights flickering, flashing turning—the moment is broken, and I'm scrambling up over prettyboy to unlatch his door, push it open, start to climb out, when the first bottle comes crashing against it, and a baseball bat *whangs* into the windshield, fracturing it, but not shattering, so that isnt the way, I fumble sideways, crawling, kick the back doors open with my good leg and come out with the aluminum bat in one hand, ready to bang the hell out of last night's bashers, who've been waiting for me all night long with their fraternity brothers and a keg of beer, the whole gang of chimpanzees, believing that I've kidnapped one of their own, they're going to rescue him from the bearded monster

except the cops are already here, beanbag rifles at the ready, lights flashing, spotlights dazzling me, the chopper above pins me in a funnel of light, so I drop the bat and raise my hands and lie down slowly on the asphalt, because already I know how this will play out

I clean up real good, no piercings, no tats, shave and a haircut, put on a clean suit, yes, I have one, but leave the prosthesis at home, fold up the pants leg, and limp into court on a crutch, tell the judge the bashers broke it when they pushed my van over, a seven-thousand dollar peg, one battered old vet with no leg to stand on, opposite a bunch of frats with attitude, there's no question what will happen here, six of them get expelled, the chapter gets its charter pulled, and the town has something to argue about until Christmas break, I'll be gone by then anyway, autumn rolls away and with it me, no more dry desert nights for this old bear, maybe I'll drift south to the tip of Baja and lie naked in the unforgiving sun like a great baking whale, or maybe north into Canada again, or Alaska, where I'll snuggle deep in a tiny cabin, hibernating like a grumpy old wolverine, listening to the snow piling up against the windows, anywhere away from here, away from the madness and the noise, the squalor of human ignorance, all the vicious scrabbling little souls that still dont get *it*, might never get it, will never get it because all the clamor they make drowns out all the other possibilities, they're screaming so loud about what they want they cant hear that the answer is already yes

when your watch says thirteen o'clock, what time is it—it's time to get a new watch, the pieces of this one are scattered all over the floor—it's time to build a new one

—something is happening, it's still happening—

All the parts of me/us, we're scattered, yes, but we're pinged and connected and we can sense/feel/hear each other. We're something new. A little two year-old girl, standing up in her crib, crying with a wet diaper, but that's not why she's crying, she's not yet ready for the burden of knowledge. A black grandmother, suddenly awake in the night, wondering why she's thinking of her dead grandson all of a sudden, he died in Nam, but she can hear him somewhere—with all time and space collapsed, he's right here now. A skinny teenage boy, secretly trying on his sister's panties, abruptly confused and wondering why he can suddenly see into the future, scared of what he's becoming and intrigued as well. The cop holding the beanbag rifle, blinking, scanning the whole situation through a dozen different pairs of eyes, instead of just his own little piece; he sees through the perp's eyes, feels the fear and terror. A young woman, screaming, channeling a joyous excruciating birth, the baby screams with her, mother and child locked together in mutual awareness. The desperate man, standing on the bridge, the choice in his eyes, suddenly alive beyond his own horizons, stepping back to reconsider. The student, looking up from his book—there's a world out there, a vast unknowable, incomprehensible world; the book, the words, the crawling insect marks upon the page, the barest shadow of meaning, there is no explanation, it's just what's happening. *Is still happening. Now.*

And all the others too, touched with wonder—frightened, intrigued, cautious, but stepping into the moment, it'll take a while. We'll get there. This thing, whatever it is we are, all of us still sorting it out, we're a long way from threshold and even farther from critical mass, we're alone, but not alone, never alone, never again.

And Michael, I glance over at him, dazed and confused, but waking up into himself now. I wonder how many more we can wake up.

British author **Tanith Lee** is one of the more celebrated authors in fantasy literature. She has published over seventy novels and 250 short stories, and has won the World Fantasy and British Fantasy Awards. "The Crow" was first published in her latest short story collection—which featured the channeled voices of Esther and Judah Garber—*Disturbed by Her Song,* a finalist for the Lambda Literary Award.

THE CROW

Judas Garbah

"Why in God's name did she call you that?"

"She hated me. I told you, she was always trying to lose me in the slums."

"Judas," said my companion, consideringly. His own name was Georges, a perfectly acceptable one. He could, if he wanted, link himself to whole calendars full of kings and saints. My name's fame, of course, came from the Iscariot family, all those years ago in Palestine. "Did you never think of changing it?"

"My father did. Once he'd extricated me from my mother's limp clutches."

"Oh? So tell me, what name did he give you?"

"Something ordinary and nondescript, a drab, paltry little name no one would remark or remember. What else but *Georges*?"

My companion then called me quite another sort of name. But presently got up and came to kiss me. A reasonably amiable lover, Georges. At least to begin with.

Soon after this, our lunch was finished. Despite the heat we rose and walked away from the terrace of the white-painted house, along the track of burnt earth that led up above the village.

A few miles off by train lay another country, and a surreal town constructed of stone vegetables, something magicked out of legend. We hadn't yet stirred ourselves to go there, too busy with ourselves and each other. But the village had begun to bore us. It was full, as all strange places are, of non-human aliens, acting out curious rituals and routines like automata. One is excluded, and anyway afraid to join in. One wishes one had gone there in disguise, able to speak in the proper local accent and dress and stink in the exact local way, so passing unobserved. But it's too late by then. One has been seen, heard, sniffed, catalogued. But then too, after all, everywhere is another planet until one has learned to know it, following which you finally understand you are *yourself* the alien, the unreal thing. Not merely uninitiated, but a monster.

Some dusty stunted olive trees cranked up the track beside us. Beyond lay emptied fields, brown vineyards already stripped of any harvest.

In a derelict poplar a cluster of black rags perched, and let out a raucous yell.

"Bloody crow," said Georges. He crouched quickly to the path, picked a shard and hurled it treeward. It seemed Georges was sullen now, not wanting this walk, but unable to decide on anything more inviting. The vegetable town, and I, the two previous attractions, must have dimmed together.

Up in the tree the crow, missed by the stone, hopped and throatily swore back at him.

Georges bent for another missile.

"Let it alone," I said, less from kindness than irritation. "It hasn't hurt you."

"I *hate* them, crows. They're bad luck." Off whirled the second stone. This one also missed. The crow however, lurched from the branches and flapped untidily off across the fields. It was old, or so it looked, its feathers dull and somehow misplaced, its chiding voice like a rusty rivet. "Go on, you devil! Get back to hell!" bellowed Georges, prancing about. He had gone mad, evidently. The red-black wine at lunch, the pale yellow spirit, the roast meat of a fresh-killed boar eaten last night, the leaky creaking house, myself, all these had driven him from his wits. My name, even, even that. How probable. Here he was, having fucked the betrayer of Christ. My God, he was doomed now all right.

At the top of the track about an hour later, we paused to regard the distant mountains, where Cathars had been hunted and tortured and burned in previous centuries. Their crime: the belief that the devil ruled the world, while God was a benign and powerless being, capable only of promising something nice after death.

Going on, appropriately perhaps, next minute a sort of wood evolved and closed in on us.

The trees were crookedly black and skeletal, strung with a bunting of dark desiccated leaves. Through their gaps the distance and its images appeared and retreated, like mosaics of vision in the henbane eater's temporary—or conclusive—blindness.

"What a spot," said Georges. "Like a witch-wood."

It was. Yet too it was the sort of terrain more normally found in northern Frankish literature. Here, it seemed a mistake. And besides, what was the type of wheedling witch who might emerge from it, to kidnap us two innocent children?

After a few more minutes of plodding on, Georges kicking at any plants on the woodland floor, the "witch" appeared.

George let out a loud silly laugh. At this, the "witch" turned all his power of attention on us. He was an old man. How old, I'm no longer certain. To me then he looked about a hundred. Very likely he was in his sixties. But in that climate, and in those days, both sexes were inclined to dry up and to desiccate, just like the distasteful leaves on the trees of the wood.

He was stooped over, very thin, all in faded black. Like the trees there, too. His hair was longish and grey. His eyes a filmy black. His nose seemed either hooked or oddly pointed. He glared at Georges, who backed away and turned to me in visible terror.

I said, in a poor facsimile of the local tongue and dialect, "Good day, señor."

At which the old bugger straightened himself, and drew from the corded belt at his waist a knife, sharp as a broken piece of glass.

~ ~ ~

Not very long ago, I was sitting on a bus in London. I do that now. Taxis are luxuries. It's Anna, sometimes Esther, who have money. Poor impoverished Judas gets by as he must, poor old dear.

But to get to the point. I found myself sitting behind another old man (I was the first) and in fact he was undoubtedly younger now than I am, in his early fifties, I'd think, maybe less.

The strangest thing instantly occurred to me. The back of his neck, the *shape* of his hair upon his head, his flat, well-made ears—these reminded me irresistibly of someone from my past, that is, my *far-off* past. A man too that I had never known well, yet somehow recalled in the most intense and—I supposed—accurate detail. For a brief while I wasn't sure whom he could be. But then gradually I remembered the witch-wood. Of course, it was none other than the "witch" himself. Had I recorded him then, so intimately, from behind—this smooth strong neck, without what my sister Anna has sometimes referred to as the 'Westerner's Crank.' That is a neck with a dent along the back of it, which describes the passage of the spine into the skull. Among male Jews, according to Anna, this indentation is always absent. I must say I've seldom ever seen it, save in adolescent boys, and certainly the man on the bus did not have this *crank*. His neck was firm and rounded as a column, crisscrossed only two or three times by a few neat horizontal creases of gathering age.

His hair was dark, but greying. His ears, I decided, were very couth, not small but neatly aligned. Nor had the lobes elongated much.

From behind, he was curiously attractive, and he had besides an appealing odor of cleanness and health, only accentuated by some powdery hint of his age. Partly I wanted to bend forward and inhale him, the nape of his neck, his greying hair. I was—to be frank—for a second aroused, in the most absurd and romantic way.

And so I recalled the one he reminded me of.

In that second too, like an omen, the bastard turned and looked out of the bus window. Not a bad face, but not the face I had unconsciously primed myself to expect. He wasn't after all the "witch" from the wood all those years before, and just above the Spanish border.

Georges screamed.

The knife in the old man's hand glittered perilously, a nasty slender penis of steel.

He stooped, and began to dig out, from under one of the trees, a clump of stiff spikes, each hosting a single indigo berry-like flower. These were, I thought, the flower known locally as *blue grape*, though I might well have mistranslated the name.

Georges tugged on my arm. "We must run away—"

"Rubbish. He isn't interested in us."

"He's mad—a madman."

The old man straightened up, at least as much as his bowed posture allowed. He shot us a glance from the drained ink of his eyes.

His free hand, which was brown and bony as a bunch of twigs, made a gesture to us. Surprisingly it was not obscene. He had beckoned. We were to follow him, somewhere. Yet his invitation seemed to give him no pleasure. He turned his back then, and stamped away among the trees.

I had spent so much of my life following unsuitable people about, often unavoidably, I immediately went after him.

Georges rambled to the rear, remonstrating, until I told him to be quiet. I thought he would leave me, believed he had, realized he had not, and partially forgot him. Our personal idyll certainly seemed to be reaching its end. Until quite mature, I tended always to expect advances—many excitable and usually unwanted—and in the same proportion, inevitable rejections. Anna used to say my own envisaging *caused* them to happen. Now I expect nothing very much, and seldom does anything come.

The sunlight burned holes through the trees, which were drawing together. Then a burnt sienna shadow, hot as a cauldron, filled the woody tunnel. Down which the old man quickly limped, illogically pursued by me (and Georges).

At the tunnel's end, a stark hillside opened out into a hole of air. Below, the wild land rolled off towards the mountains. On the brink, like something washed up by a wave, stood an old-fashioned house of some size and dilapidation. Before it was a yard, with chickens picking about, or squawking and flapping up on the broken wall. A line of red jars stood there, and fallen all around were bits of tiles from the roof. The old man, not once looking back, crossed the yard, cursing the chickens in thickly ornamental vernacular. He thrust at a wooden door, already ajar, and lurched on into the silent cavern of this palatial hovel.

"Don't," said Georges, running to catch me. "Don't be *stupid,* Judas."

I shook him off, navigated the chickens, and also walked straight into the house.

It was instantly underwater cool. So many of those places are like this inside their cave walls of stone. The space was wide, the floor also laid with tiles, also broken. A stair curved out of it, leading to the upper story.

But a deeper shadow was in charge there, and the sickly honeyish smell of warmed rot drifted down.

Georges had now entered too, and fidgeted behind me.

"Those jars left outside are full of *piss*," he informed me.

"It's probably stale wine," I said. "Unless he's a tanner."

"Oh don't be such a fool, Judas. Let's get out."

The old man in black had disappeared, and there was a choice as to where he might have gone. Undoubtedly not up the stair so fast. But three closed doors marked the stained, veined empty walls, and a single archway, that gave on a steeply angled passage. Some sense of light was there.

A svelte lizard ran over the tiles on little clicking feet.

Georges now shrieked. He wasn't afraid of lizards.

I turned round, and saw a short round woman, covered up in the familiar drained black. She must have come in from outside as we had, and seemed furious rather than startled by our presence. At noisy Georges in particular she cast a baleful look, and spat directly on the floor, presumably either to ill wish him, or to render him invisible. As neither spell seemed to take, she briskly clumped across to one of the three doors, went through and slammed it.

Georges wailed as I progressed into the angled passage. Its crooked arm led out into another high-walled area, this roofless and lit by the open sky. It was a courtyard, once carefully planted, now becoming ruinous. Small stretched dead trees and roping brown vines webbed the walls, in some of them little mummified fruits, unrecognizable and black. A dry fountain had a noseless cherub pouring nothing from a shell. The floor was beaten earth, sun baked, and scattered by what looked like the torn-off wings of insects scorched in fire. He, the old man, sat on a stone bench against the wall. He too looked scorched, if not quite mummified.

He glanced at me again.

"*Inglés*," he said.

I smiled. "No."

His eyes, tarnished mirrors. "*Judio*," he accurately decided.

I added, "*Mitad árabe.*"

He showed his tarnished teeth, a grin, or a primeval signal of rage, and lowered his gaze to the fistful of blue grape he was busy thrusting into soil.

The sun was slanting over. A ray struck suddenly down on the court, hitting the edge of the dead fountain. A strange noise sounded. I stared transfixed.

Very slowly, the wrecked cherub was splitting into two. As the two halves (perhaps like me, one half Jew, one half Arab) folded back, a peculiar black creature slid out. It most resembled a salamander, a tiny dragon from some bestiary. Huge barbs or spines ran along the ridge of its back. A pair of stiff black wings stiffly rose up, the hinged jaw undid and out came a violent hissing that made me jump. It wasn't I'd thought the thing was alive, I knew it must only be some mechanism, but the noise was vicious and I had no idea what to anticipate from it next. It showed me. Out of the clockwork jaws rushed a glittering stream of dirty fluid that splashed about the basin and over on to the earth below. The emission ceased. The mouth clapped shut with a clank.

The old man was laughing, presumably at me. I took no notice and went to inspect the salamander, now it was still. It seemed made of black iron. Had the sun shaft activated it? Maybe. Or else some trigger under the bench where the old man might tap it with his foot.

Behind me, back in the house, I could hear a murmur of voices. One seemed to belong to Georges, who had not come with me into the court.

"He is in no true danger from Marija," said the old man, in the local polyglot. I had begun to detect the more strident tones of a woman. Marija, then. She was welcome to Georges.

The old man had potted up the blue grape, and now, alarmingly, he came across the court towards me. He walked like a crab, arrogantly limping almost sideways. His face was made of brown pleatings. He leant past me and rapped the dragon on its snout. At which it raised itself all the way up on to its hind limbs, like a dog begging. It had eyes of mica that flashed. "Made of me. I am," the old man said to me, with a terrible, implacable pride, "Cuerca. Patxi Cuerca. Come, I will show you, in my room."

In the house, Georges was hysterically protesting in French, "*Non, non, madame—*"

But had he been in the court with us probably he would have clung to me, trying to anchor me to the spot, and save me from who knew what worse-than-death fate the old man was plotting.

Unimpeded, I accompanied Patxi Cuerca. And what sort of name was that, if I had even understood him? *Cuerca*—didn't that mean *crow*? Or no, perhaps not. Yet he was like a crow, like the eldritch crow in the tree the two stones missed.

The Room led directly off the court. Through the round-topped door we entered a windowless blank, where something seemed lurking in a smell of spice and mould. He struck a match and lit a lantern which hung just inside. I had not even seen it. Then, he shut us in.

A child somewhere—where? who?—had told me about the chamber in the rock where the robbers hid their treasure and Ali Baba found it. The child had not been Anna, though she was quite capable of that. But my sisters and I had never met when we were children.

The lantern, a huge ungainly object, swung for a few moments, then settled itself.

It was a filthy room, into which a rainbow had fallen, splashing everywhere, even into the webs of spiders.

With the erosion of time, which can eat at the edges even of the most visual memory, Cuerca's Room is difficult to describe, at least in logical terms. It acted instead on the optic nerve, the viscera.

What did I see first? There was a stripe of pure green that hung and blazed as if with green fire, and rippled as if with green water. And over there, another stripe, this one orange, that did similar things. And there was a crimson square that kept immobile and glowed like the core of a hearth. And curves of deep blue and purple that twitched and waited, and a slinking manipulative yellow, like a leopard.

He didn't advise me. He let me find my own way. I began to see in greater depth.

He, it could only have been he, had painted shapes on the walls in vivid opaque color. And over them and beside them and before them had been hung or slung, or nailed, or simply piled, objects that were of those same colors, either exactly, or in some corresponding color-echo. A bunch of green enamel grapes suspended from a green cord before the green stripe, an emerald glass pitcher, its neck smashed off and instead surmounted with a green-painted egg, stood below, jade grapes on a plate of green faint enough to seem transparent. Against the red oblong rags of a tattered vermilion banner from some war, a red cup holding an artificial rose like blood. Where the yellow uncoiled, a piece of ochre ivory, shaped like the fretboard from some giant's guitar, nestled in a cascade of broken yellow glass. Against the blue a woman's blue shoe, its little heel caught in a sapphire comb. A cluster of dried oranges choked by necklaces of chipped amber melted into the orange circle…

The old man, Cuerca, went by me, and unceremoniously and unerringly shoved the purplish grape-flowers between the violet colored jug without a handle and the chunk of raw amethyst beside the hoop of purple paint.

The expensive and the worthless clustered in each group as one. No hierarchies among these items, lost or abandoned, stolen or thrown out on rubbish heaps, all eventually pilfered by him, by Patxi Cuerca, brought here and each made part of its correct entity.

To outline all this is only to invite incomprehension and scorn. How could such an eccentric, *childish* medley convey anything? It did. No doubt the dark, flooded selectively by the big cracked lantern, caused some of the effect. But that hot day maybe my eyes had been thirsty. And now they drank.

The lamp flickered, some insect or cobweb dropping in there. I saw the yellow shape, crusted with its glisten, swing quietly sidelong to seize the blue shape—a woman, dancing—in its mouth. How gracefully she fell. But the red shape, stretching from oblong to square, and back to oblong, sprouted a thousand red roses, twining and knotting with their ruby thorns. The purple shape was a galleon's sail, marked with an indecipherable device. The orange shape was the ship's bodywork. They flowed together and sailed over the green shape of sea, which spangled and rioted with darting jade fish, spraying up the emerald foam—

But I thought of the spice and mold I could still smell, of drugs grown and harvested from the petrified courtyard, which formerly had been, had it, a Garden of Earthly Delights?

I blinked, once, twice. The shapes were static. Almost. Priceless and worthless. Unalive and living. They only shimmered a little, as the lamp had. Flicked a blue sequined eyelid or a sinuous tail. One last minuscule wave broke over the amber figurehead, who pursed her lips, before her face lapsed back to necklaces. The purple sail shivered as it flattened out against the wall. A single petal fell through the roses. Became again a broken red bead.

Quite suddenly then the old man, the magician, turned round, and the finale of his magic show was accomplished.

I saw him dazzling clear, meshed between the streams and orifices of colors. Like the salamander which had emerged from the chipped cherub, the real man now stepped free of his shell. Cuerca was young. He was straight, tall, lean, his shoulders back, his body planted as fluidly as an athlete's on his strong long legs. He wore his now inky clothes only in affectation, to match the ink-black feathers of his thick smooth hair, the jet stones of his eyes. His unlined face was handsome, nose aquiline, mouth long, slender and aloof. In his beautiful hands, articulately strong enough to rip out any beating heart, he held a burnished flame of knife. But you could not be afraid at this. You wanted all, and therefore anything and everything he might do. And he said to me, in perfect, only-slightly accented French (while the light glinted on his white teeth), "Go along now. Get out. You've seen. Go and rescue your friend from Marija. *Remember.* I am Patxi Cuerca. Never *forget* you have seen me, and this room."

And then, weightless and careless, as if casting a paper, he tossed the knife over my head. It thunked into some soft place in the wall behind me.

Disarranged by its motion, the lamplight jumped again, the rainbow leapt, and all its pieces, with the shadow, came down on him, and covered him up. He was old once more, dirty and crippled, and crazy. So I turned and went out, and in the courtyard the dragon too had slid back into its stony carapace. The liquid it had spat was already dry.

~ ~ ~

Although I rescued him from Marija, Georges did not forgive me. She had been telling him he was her long lost son, it seemed, and threatening him with the rich (seventeen olive trees) betrothed he had deserted, telling him she would bring him wine and he must drink it.

Perhaps he *was* her son. After all, I had seen the Room, and I had seen Cuerca grow young again, and then old again. Metamorphosis riddled the place.

No doubt Cuerca's youth was only a trick of the light, as they say. Or drugs burning. Or the dazzling after-images of all the colors sprawled about in there.

Around thirteen years later—also long ago now—I saw a photograph of him as a young man, in a book to do with the art of that torrid southern region. For of course he had been an artist of repute, when young. Abstract paintings, sculptures and mechanical toys not for children, peculiar gardens even, were credited to his invention. He did, in the picture, look remarkably like what I'd glimpsed, or imagined, standing among his last creation, his Room. (The book did not mention, or did not know about, the Room.) But probably, even by the time I opened the book and saw him there, he was himself dead.

As Georges and I tramped back to our rented house in the ash of the afternoon, he swore at me and I at him. Any liking was gone, and any tenderness. Which wouldn't, naturally, prevent an orgy of famished coupling for another two days and three nights.

When we passed below the poplar tree, the crow had returned there. It sat far up, raising its disheveled head to the over-gilded sky and rasping out a succession of caws.

Georges at once transferred his vitriol, or some of it, to the crow. "If I had a gun I'd shoot it!" And then to me, "I'd shoot you too, you damned Semite bugger."

But I only saw Cuerca's knife as if skimmed over my head; *Remember me. Remember me.*

Georges, immune to his own repetitions, was scrabbling for another stone. I pushed him hard so he fell flat on the track. When he got up, he followed me in rebellious docility.

"Bloody crow," he muttered. "Crow-crow-crow. Why do you want to protect it? What use is it? It's old and diseased and worthless. It's nothing."

The crow lifted itself out of the quills of the poplar. It spread its wings and sprang into the sky.

"Look, Georges," I said. "Do you see? It can fly."

From a fragmentary MS by Judas Garbah, collated and adapted by Anna Garber, his sister.

Steve Berman has been writing queer and weird fiction for many years. He has been a finalist for the Andre Norton Award, the Golden Crown Literary Award and the Lambda Literary Award. He is working on a collection of young adult stories, new fairy tales for queer youth. He lives in southern NJ with his feline familiar and guardian, Daulton.

Tell Me What You Love, and I'll Tell You What You Are

Steve Berman

I WANT YOU TO ask yourself a question at the end of this story.

As a kid, I spent many weekend afternoons, regardless of the weather, in front of the television. UHF existed then as a range of wondrous and obsolescent movies and programming, and Saturdays were devoted to long hours still dressed in pajamas and discovering whether channel 17 or 48 had the better horror film.

One film, a Hammer film, *Vampire Circus*, I shall never forget because of this scene:

Two sons of a prominent villager are drawn by their curiosity to the site of the gypsy circus. Not some paltry bit of showmanship

I WANT YOU TO wonder which side is true.

I know I was thirteen when I first watched *Vampire Circus* because I masturbated to that scene for weeks afterwards. My face pressed against the mattress as I would grind my bared crotch against a soft clump of bedding gathered in the eager moments beforehand.

I would recast the scene with me facing the handsome acrobat. His smirk daring me to go further than I had ever dreamt with another boy. His billowy shirt is open at the neck, yet not open wide enough for me to see his chest. I ache to see an expanse of ivory-hued pectoral muscle and the terrain of exposed ribs.

surrounding a squeezebox, a dancing bear and a fortune teller, but a grand, debauched spectacle of painted faces, velvet curtains and a Hall of Mirrors. I suspect the boys' father must have warned them against going, because why else would they have come alone? (The older brother was the same age as that teenage Steve sitting in front of the television set.) A pair of vampiric acrobats awaits the boys among the mirrors. The brothers are enchanted, lured inside through a pane of cold glass. The rakish male acrobat guides the older boy with a light touch on his chin, as if holding something so precious. Then blood is spilt.

His fingers chill but soft as they tug at my chin and pull me Inside. I shudder. He doesn't need to mesmerize me but he does. My eyes stay open, focused on the darkness around us as he bares his fangs.

Most nights I never make it to the moment he bites me but collapse, semen spilling and staining the sheets, while still staring into his gaze.

But now and then I feel the sting of his mouth.

My nephew came out to me a few days after his sixteenth birthday. I suspected, of course, but never wanted to rush him from the closet.

My nephew is in denial. He is a bear cub. The endomorphic build. He has more hair on his back at sixteen than I ever will. It's a pelt. But he falls for slivers masquerading as boys. Somehow their disguise demands tight jeans and many string or rubber bracelets.

I worry I might be turning into a bear. Not the animal, but the heavy-set and hirsute gay man.

I see my nephew's ignorance about his physicality and remember that when I was his age I weighed 110 lbs. I was a sliver masquerading as a boy myself. Now, more than twice my nephew's age, I find myself confronting an expanding waistline, hairs growing where I wish they wouldn't, and, I must admit, realizing some attraction for the same.

A carnival has come to southern New Jersey, and my sister has asked me to chaperone a sort-of date between my nephew and one bleached blond sophomore.

On the ride to the fairgrounds, the boys occupy the back seat of my Stanza with laughter and text messages.

The parking lot is gravel. The sophomore leans out the car window and clears his throat a moment before spitting out the dust hanging low in the air. My nephew takes note and makes sure to step on the very spot where the boy's saliva darkens the ground. I wonder about this sympathetic magic of his.

Circus peanuts make me think of semen.

In college, I was in love, or maybe lust, with my roommate. He had a sweet tooth, and so I plied his affections with bags of candy. But he was straight, and my syrupy, saccharine intentions failed to change him.

One morning, after my roommate drove home his latest girlfriend, I came out to find on the edge of the trashcan an empty bag of circus peanuts and a full, used condom.

Spongy, orange circus peanuts do not taste like…well, real peanuts. My roommate's semen, my first real taste of a man, had a bitter flavor. I've never grown reconciled to it.

The sun is starting to set and the horizon could be burning.

Just beyond the ticket booth, the midway, with its flashing lights, chimes and bells and shouts, cloying smells like popcorn and hot funnel cake, calls to us.

My nephew insists on buying the blond sophomore's ticket. The gesture makes me proud.

Near the gate a young girl is selling roses.

"Do they still sell roses on Valentine's Day at the high school?" I ask my nephew.

He nods.

"Back in my day, you never dared send a flower to another guy."

The blond sophomore looks back at me. "Was there a boy you wanted to give a rose to?"

"Yeah. And more than a few I wished would send me one."

Then my nephew says, "They've bred all the perfume out of roses."

Every man has sniffed his own armpit and will do so on and off throughout his life. Some, like me, I must admit, cannot resist inhaling deeply, an act of self-awareness as simple yet intimate as checking a pulse.

Do vampires have a scent? Didn't Stoker write that Dracula's breath reeked of the grave? I suspect in films these days the undead don't reek like their distant cousins, the walking dead.

I have heard there exists in Moscow a darkened and indulgent brothel that blindfolds its patrons, wealthy men and women, and makes them choose their whore wholly by sense of smell.

I imagine myself at such a venue. Stripped-down men are brought before me to offer their chests, their armpits, their necks for me to sniff as if I were a connoisseur of such things. Perhaps I am. I know some smoke Habanos cigars, and some wear drops of cologne, while others have been instructed not to bathe. There will be that one who has so refrained for days, all the while exerting himself until his skin is steeped in his own musk. And I would nod, selecting him without ever knowing his physique. Or face.

There is a handsome guy working the Guess Your Weight, Your Age, Your Fate booth. He wears seersucker shorts and a yellow polo shirt, and he's reclining in a high-backed chair upholstered in checkered aqua and lemon squares.

As we walk past—the boys chomping at cotton candy tufts, me eating a corn dog—the guy lifts one leg like a pointer and calls out:

"Guess your weight," to my nephew, whose eyes widen; "Guess your age," to the blond sophomore, who's so startled he drops his treat; "Guess your fate," to me. The guy ends with a toothy grin intended for one and all.

I can't walk away from such a claim and, even if the boys don't want to play along, I pop the corn dog into my mouth and put a hand at both their t-shirt collars to slow them down. One finger sinks into my nephew's back pelt.

In the film, the boys attacked by the vampiric acrobat were waifs. The acrobat, himself, thanks to a liquid crimson diet, could best be described as lithe. I have a paunch these days. Paunch. Monosyllabic words are so easy on the ear. It sounds almost alluring, far better than some stomached synonyms.

I'm no longer the same age as that boy victim. I'm older than the toothy acrobat, too. Why does he benefit from never aging, and I must face my reflection in the bathroom mirror, face the gray hairs. Not yet in my pubes, but one day I'll find them there…

I worry that I'll end up alone.

When I hand the handsome guy a crumpled ten dollar bill to have our mass/years/fortune revealed, his fingers linger over mine. I find his gaze captivating…

…I cannot speak for a few seconds: a rarity.

The guy stands up with a sudden but smooth push against the chair's arms. "So, you," the guy says to my nephew, "are one point seven qantars." The man slaps my nephew on the back. "Not bad, not bad. A little light on the steppes."

"What did he say?" my nephew asks.

"And you…" The handsome guy has already turned to the blond. He leans in close and sniffs at the boy's t-shirt (stenciled *Pennsylvania Route 420*). "Definitely Age of Aquarius."

That makes the sophomore blink. "I—I don't get it. I'm that lion."

"And me?" I ask.

"Ten dollars poorer." He winks at me.

Teenage boys love to laugh whenever an adult is fooled.

I like words. Obviously. I especially like words during sex. *Wordsduringsex* would be more apt, an admission spent in one moan, one breath.

But I've never been to bed with another guy who understands what I want, what I need said to me. Like a secret incantation to open my heart.

The blond sophomore asks my nephew to reach new heights atop the Ferris wheel.

The carny working the controls, a tan woman with a lot of those free pens banks give away shoved through her dreadlocks, sees my fearful appraisal. "Relax. It's a Troposphere. They made 'em great in the fifties. Decommissioned naval steel."

I watch as she guides the boys into a gondola. My nephew's nose wrinkles at her smell. The blond sophomore sees the expression and chuckles.

The safety bar she shoves in place does little to fend off a sudden bout of acrophobia as the mechanism grunts with power and I watch the boys ascend.

Better for me to hunt down whatever the small carnival has to offer in the way of mirrors.

Not too far off I find a trailer painted midnight blue and covered in used picture frames. Puffy, airbrushed lettering on two sides reads *Mirrorville*.

Should a Hall of Mirrors be conveyable?

After I give the wizened "Mayor of Mirrorville" my ticket, he welcomes me to town, which is narrow, dark, and has sticky pavement. And a population of just three.

Shouldn't you remember your first date? But I don't.

I remember the first kiss. A desperate fool, I bestowed it on the first guy who showed any interest in me. Given and soon regretted when we went further than we should have. I've told the story before, how he transformed before my eyes from attractive to repulsive in a matter of moments. Like a movie monster.

I envy my nephew, who has the chance to make memories that will not haunt him.

The first mirror, fashioned from a thick slab of silvered glass and atop a cement pedestal, disappoints: I see my reflection and nothing else. A sudden frustration fills my limbs with lead and even shuffling my feet as I stand there, staring at myself, is effort.

To my right, the second mirror looks like an antique. I see my nephew and the blond sophomore sitting in their gondola. They are kissing and my heart swells… (lub) with affection (dub) with regret over how long I had to wait before I had that perfect moment.

The third mirror is situated at the very end of the corridor, a round, elaborately gilt-framed pane. I have to walk close to peer at the glass.

On the floor of my parents' den, the older boy from Vampire Circus sits in familiar pajamas and eats a peanut butter and jelly sandwich while watching the movie on the massive television set. On the cathode screen, a fourteen-year-old me is leading a brother I never had into the gypsy's Hall of Mirrors.

I suck in a breath. I am terrified and excited, expecting to see the deadly acrobat come for me. I feel someone moving behind me.

I turn around and there's the handsome guy from the Guess Your Weight, Your Age, Your Fate booth. He slips that ten dollar bill into my

Last Halloween, I tried to find a husband in the mirror.

A tattered book promised this was possible, and I had grown up trusting books rather than people. I'm so lonely that even superstition has become promising.

If that night, I walked backwards through the house, up the staircase without care, then I needed only to look in a hand mirror by candlelight and I'd see my future husband's face over my shoulder.

There was a risk. All magic has to have risk. Instead of his face, I might see a grisly visage and I'd die before meeting anyone.

The rite had been only intended for girls, so I enacted some small changes for my needs.

As I walked through the house, I undressed, as if coming home to an eager lover. I faced forwards rather than backwards; I'm no longer in the closet, I have no reason to take any steps back. And the mirror I used was, well, the medicine cabinet because I don't own a hand mirror. But there were lit Yankee Candles, scented like pumpkin pie, because I suspect my future husband might be a bear.

Suppose I saw teeth?

front pocket, a gesture both kind and alluring.

"A refund?" I ask.

He shakes his head. His smile, though toothy, is sweet. "Think of this as guaranteeing satisfaction," he tells me.

I wonder if that boy from the film was watching me now.

Jameson Currier is the author of the novels *Where the Rainbow Ends* and *The Wolf at the Door* and four collections of short fiction: *Dancing on the Moon; Desire, Lust, Passion, Sex; Still Dancing: New and Selected Stories;* and *The Haunted Heart and Other Tales*. "July 2002" is the opening chapter of his most recent novel, *The Third Buddha.*

July 2002

Jameson Currier

"I'm not convinced two men can have an honest relationship," I said. I had not said anything at all during dinner, remaining quiet and listening to the mix of political and sexual banter bounce between the other guests and our hosts, as Eric delivered one elaborately prepared dish after another to the table. My neighbors Eric and his lover Sean, a gay couple in their mid-fifties, threw little soirées biweekly in their Chelsea apartment for a combination of their single and coupled gay friends, in order to be matchmakers or therapists as the necessity of their friendships required. I was twenty-four that summer and staying in my older brother's apartment down the hall; it was often impossible to escape Eric's attentions as I came and went from the building, and I once amusingly accused him of installing a spy cam because he was so knowledgeable of my comings and goings—or lack thereof—particularly my desire for hibernating for long stretches on the sofa watching movie after movie, the titles of which he also seemed to know.

But it was my comment on the inadequacies of gay relationships that immediately stirred up my host that evening.

"Of course they can!" Eric answered me. "You've just had a bad experience." And then to his other guests: "Teddy is just talking nonsense. He's too young to really believe that."

"Think about it," I continued. "Two men. In a relationship. How much truth can there be?"

"As much as you can accept," Eric answered. "Not every relationship is the same. And sometimes just because a man has secrets, doesn't mean that he is not an honest man and truthful to his partner. Sometimes it's a matter of compromise, not truth."

"Maybe you just haven't met the right man," Stan said to me. Stan was a friend of a friend of Eric's. He worked in a foreign-service program and had returned to the States and New York because of "family business," which none of us had asked him to elaborate on, respectfully considering it another off-topic issue that evening. "Family business" could mean either a parent's illness or a sibling's marriage or divorce. Or it could be a deeper secret, a way to disguise one's own truth. Perhaps Stan had been in some kind of legal or financial trouble. Perhaps he was bisexual and married and had a child—or had fathered an illegitimate one. It was a mystery Stan was not ready to explain or reveal to anyone that evening.

But I was grateful that I didn't have to elaborate any further on my own disastrous personal experiences and that the others around the dining table were now drawn into the conversation.

"Or perhaps you're too focused on sex being an equivalent of love," Sean said to me, jokingly. Sean was a psychiatrist, so everyone always gave his words more weight than those of his stockier partner, though Eric, a respected commercial photographer, relished being the foolish and more socially frivolous of the two. "I certainly had that problem when I was your age," Sean added. "Of course, I'm wiser now because my sex drive is not what it once was. But I don't think that sex should be the sole basis of a long-term relationship with another man. Too much disappointment."

"Are you saying I'm not sexy?" Eric whined across the table. "Or lousy in bed?"

This was followed by nervous laughter from everyone.

"Of course, as Eric said, every relationship is distinct," Sean added.

I was glad the topic soon shifted back to Stan, who until recently had worked in Afghanistan, and as dinner progressed from drinks to salad to entrees to dessert, the tale of Stan's work in a clinic in the Bamiyan province unraveled as he recounted his experience aiding a television journalist who had been injured in an accident. The journalist was a mutual friend of Eric and Sean. And in the odd set of connections and circumstances of those at dinner that evening, the journalist Stan had helped had once lived in my brother's apartment, before my brother had assumed the lease. Eric was particularly proud that he was able to join together all the pieces of this puzzle over a three-course meal.

I was tired that evening and after a rich and heavy dessert of Dutch apple pie and ice cream, I excused myself from the party and the other guests and went back to my apartment. I had found it increasingly difficult to be social with other guys, which Eric had noted, of course, and which had been the catalyst for the dinner invitation. That week I was also watching another neighbor's dog, Joe's black cocker spaniel named Inky, while Joe was away in Los Angeles. Inky was a beautiful dog, a princess who padded about softly and tossed her curly head and floppy ears at me; one of her unacknowledged blessings was that she pulled me in and out of the apartment so that I did not completely lose contact with the outside world. I was greeted with a whoosh of affection as I stepped through the apartment door, tiny paws landing just below the faded white of the knees of my jeans. I snapped on her leash and we went to the end of the hallway to wait for the building's sluggishly slow-arriving elevator.

As it finally arrived, Stan was leaving Eric and Sean's apartment and I held the elevator door open while he said good-bye to the two men with handshakes and kissed cheeks. He joined me for the ride to the ground floor and Inky's brisk sprint through the lobby to the sidewalk.

I liked Stan. Unlike our hosts, who were forever filling empty spaces with nonsensical chatter and opinions, he was not much of a talker. He was a tall, handsome, masculine man, a guy's guy who always seemed to be well put together and admired, about three or four years older than I was, so I felt a more generational bonding with him than I had shared with our older hosts, who had, in the eleven months I had lived in my brother's apartment, tried to step into the roles of mentor, parent or guide for me. There was also a quiet modesty to Stan, as evinced by the personal story he would not disclose at dinner—he had been as vague in many of his statements as I was that evening about my ruinous love life—and there had been not an ounce of bravado when he had recounted his assistance to Eric's friend in Afghanistan. I admired the fact that he had boldly stepped into foreign service after graduating college, something I had not been able to do myself, and I envied him for having already amassed a handful of anecdotal adventures that he could recount to strangers over a meal. But it had also made me feel rather inconsequential in the fabric of gay life and that perhaps I had been wasting my life in the city. In the elevator I was bashfully shy—or rudely uninterested in him—but Stan gruffly complimented Inky's beauty and funneled me questions about her and her owner which kept both of us looking down at the curly black mop of her and not at each other.

It was a warm summer night, mid-July, and the day's heat still seemed trapped close to the sidewalk. I broke into a light sweat as I moved away from the air-conditioning of the building and into the city air. We walked silently together to the end of the block and were about to shake hands as we reached Eighth Avenue where Stan would head towards the subway stop to begin his journey back to Long Island.

On the street, a bike messenger—an Asian guy about our age in a tank top and bright green cycling shorts—suddenly rode across a pothole he had not seen in his path. He went flying over the handlebars and landed on the street, unconscious. From the angle where we were standing we had both witnessed the accident. The messenger had not been wearing a helmet for protection. Stan touched me on the shoulder as the guy was rising up in the air, over the handlebars of the bike and onto the pavement, as if to keep me in place and out of harm, and once the fellow had landed on the ground, Stan rushed into the street to aid him.

"Do you have a cell phone?" There was already blood on his shirt from where he had leaned into the Asian boy's head to check his wound.

I did, but not with me. I stepped farther away from Stan and the accident and stopped another guy who was walking by and talking on a cell phone, and I tapped him on the shoulder and asked, "Could you call nine-one-one for us?"

He was a beefy sort of guy, wearing a formfitting T-shirt and carrying a shoulder bag, and I gathered he must have just been at one of the gyms that dotted the neighborhood. He nodded at me, hung up on his call, and called the emergency line and explained to the operator where we were.

Before he had hung up, a police car arrived, followed by an ambulance, and soon the messenger was being lifted onto a stretcher.

I thanked the beefy guy, and he disappeared as the officers and emergency workers arrived, and Inky's restlessness tugged me to one end of the block and back so she could sniff around and do her business.

When the ambulance and officers left and the street was cleared of gawkers, it was just Stan and myself and the dog. Stan's clothes were soiled and his hands were dirty with grime and dried blood. The messenger would be all right—more blood and broken bones than serious internal damages, the medical workers seemed to think. His blackout had only been for a minute or so. But he was being taken to the hospital for stitches and further tests.

"You can't get on the subway like that," I said to Stan. "You can wash up and take one of my brother's shirts."

We walked back to the apartment building and self-consciously waited for the elevator. I tried to commend Stan on his quick actions, but it felt strained and awkward and I was tired and ready to be on my own for the night, and Inky was restlessly tugging at the leash because she knew she would soon get a treat when we were back in the apartment.

In the elevator I unhooked Inky's leash and she leapt down the hall when we reached my floor. Inside the apartment, I pointed to the bathroom—the layout was not much different from Eric and Sean's apartment—and went to give Inky a treat and then find a shirt for Stan to wear.

A few minutes later he emerged bare chested and asked if I had a plastic bag he could use to carry his soiled clothes back to Long Island. It was impossible not to take in his body's military athleticism—thick, muscled shoulders and arms and a nicely developed chest covered with black hair curving into a thin, dark line that traveled down the middle of his solid stomach and widened again above his navel. I handed him the shirt I had found in my brother's closet and went into the kitchen to find a bag.

Stan was in the living room wearing my brother's shirt when I handed him the plastic bag and, as he stuffed the soiled clothes inside it, he asked, "Do you think they were trying to set us up?"

"I know for a fact that they were trying to set us up."

He nodded and smiled and stepped a little closer to where I was standing.

"You're a nice guy," he complimented me. "It would be a shame to disappoint them."

I smiled and bowed my head, accepting the approval, and he kissed me on my forehead.

He was a big guy and it was a brotherly gesture, but it made me feel vulnerable. I lifted my eyes up to him, which was when his kiss fell against my lips.

Slowly, clumsily, as if being awakened from a deep sleep, I put my arms around his waist. His hands slipped around me and settled at the belt loops of my jeans, where he hooked his fingers as I moved my hands beneath his shirt and around to his chest. I had wanted to kiss him since I had met him at Eric and Sean's and I held my lips open as he forcefully moved his tongue into my mouth, as if to prove that he had been interested in me, after all.

He tugged the bottom of my T-shirt and slid it up over my arms and tossed it behind him, and his hands moved to my waist as he pressed his mouth against the center of my chest. His lips rode up my neck and I let him linger there till the pleasure was unbearable, and then I took the edges of his shirt and pulled them towards his head.

We stood bare chested now in front of each other, deep-tonguing and stroking each other's bodies. I rubbed his nipple between my thumb and forefinger while he moved a hand to my crotch and grasped the erection beneath my jeans. Then he unzipped my fly, pressed his hand inside and clutched my cock through the fabric of my underwear.

My hands moved to unbutton the top of his khaki pants and as the zipper gave way his trousers fell off his hips and puddled at his knees. He was wearing a pair of light blue boxers, tented from the head of his cock, and I reached my hand to his thigh and slipped my fingers under the hem of his boxers until I found its wide, mushroom-shaped head. His cock was warm and hard and I clutched it and gave a few strokes, then found his testicles and cupped and squeezed them.

He pulled away from me as if to find his balance and breath, and I took the opportunity to slip out of my jeans. He sat on the arm of the couch and undid the laces of his shoes and stepped out of his trousers. He had a nice smile and I leaned over him and kissed him, and we fondled each other for another few moments, then I drew him up by his arms and he followed me into the bedroom.

We were rougher now, stroking, kissing, tweaking, nibbling. In the darkness of the bedroom I could see his smile and he made soft noises of astonishment as we twisted and rolled around. I expected him to withdraw from my rising intensity, but he accepted it and pushed it farther. I wanted him to love me because I found him, in spite of whatever secrets he might possess, a good, honest man—and to love him in a way that could transcend the need for sex but would also embrace its deepest desires. I thought that if I could prove to him that I was a good sexual partner then he would also see that I could be a good boyfriend or husband for him, a mistake I continually made with every man I found my way into a bedroom with.

He asked if I had lube and condoms, and I rolled away from him and found them in the drawer of the nightstand. I thought he wanted to fuck me, but it was the opposite. I took it slow, fingering him till he was ready to accept my cock. He gasped and his chest flushed as I entered him and I pulled out until he hungrily urged me back. He wanted to hold my neck as I fucked him and I obliged until I realized I could curve my spine and take his cock in my mouth as I remained inside him. I felt entirely innocent and genuine with him, as if this were the first time I had ever done this with a guy and we were to do this together the rest of our lives. He was full of puffs of astonishment and I could feel the muscles of his stomach clenching and shifting and I kept at him, unrelenting.

He pushed my lips away as his orgasm arrived and I withdrew from him and finished myself off. I left him and toweled myself off in the bathroom, regarding the satisfaction of my smile and the raw, red patches on my shoulders and neck where the stubble of his jaw had burned my skin. Back at the bed, Stan toweled himself off, and there followed a long period of lying together cuddling, holding each other, rubbing our hands and fingers along skin and hair. I mentally reprimanded myself for pushing myself so emotionally into the sex and for stepping into what I really knew was to be another one-night stand. I knew it wouldn't go any farther with Stan than this pleasurable moment, and I felt the hurt and disappointment of it before he had even left the apartment.

"You must have been starved for affection there," I said, as I lifted myself out of his embrace, referring to his time working in Afghanistan.

"No," he answered. "Just the opposite. There was a local boy," he said, then quickly clarified, "...young man. He was a handsome young man."

He rolled over so that he looked out the window, away from me, and I followed him, wrapping my arms around his waist in an effort to keep us together. I could feel his voice vibrating through his skin and into my fingers as he talked. "It began innocently enough. Eye contact. Flirting. Holding hands."

"Holding hands?" I said and lightly laughed.

"Casually," he explained. "It's a gesture of friendship between men. Muslim men are openly affectionate towards each other in a way that would be regarded as odd—or gay—here, and it's easy to fall into their habits.

"I was working at the clinic," he said, after a pause, as if he had been reviewing a memory before he attempted to describe it. "Dispensing medicines at the makeshift pharmacy. Tending to walk-in emergencies. Trying to patch up all these problems with aspirin and Band-Aids."

Now he laughed as I had, lightly, then continued. "The young boy showed up one day looking for work. I shooed him away because there was nothing for him to do but get in the way, and there was nothing to pay him with. But he returned about an hour later. He was really looking for food and I gave him some bread and a chocolate bar I had saved since I was in Kabul. He was ecstatic. He knew a little English. They all know a little English there."

"Hello, Meesturh," Stan mimicked the accent. "I lihcke you. You lihcke me?"

We both laughed at the imitation, and Stan continued. "Like I said, it started with flirting. He was always smiling at me and he had a terrific smile—dimples on his left cheek you just wanted to drop your tongue into. He was always happy to help me with whatever I was doing. He made me smile. I gave him food every day. Bread I had taken from the guesthouse where I was staying and taking my meals. I would be grumpy in the mornings until he showed up, ravenous, and I watched him eat. He was sleeping in the caves up on the cliffs."

"The caves?"

"The grottoes on the hillside, carved by the Buddhist monks centuries ago. Where the ancient giant Buddhas had been. They were cold, nasty places, and I have no idea how he stayed warm at night, because it could get very cold. There were many families living in the caves and I can only imagine that their body heat was what was warming them—when they had food to fill their stomachs. The boy had been separated from his parents at a refugee camp, and he was staying with his older sister's family—her husband and a little baby girl. He was tall and slender, bony from hunger, as if you could see him growing right before your eyes into a hungry young man. He wouldn't eat all the food that I gave him. There was always something that he tucked away in his pocket that I knew he would give to one of them later. It was heartbreaking if you stopped to think of it, but there was so much to think about, that this was only one minor thing. Every day there was another casualty or a patient with a problem—an abscessed tooth or a broken toe. *Something*. It was such a cold, harsh place. Beautiful. But *hard*."

He continued. "One night I was able to bring him to the guesthouse to dine. It was owned by a local Muslim man and he had always objected to my suggestion of the boy eating with us, in spite of my offer to pay extra to have him there, then one night the owner changed his mind. The boy ate with us—the rest of the MSF staff in the clinic and a few of the Red Cross guys who were also in the house—and they all knew him and were glad to have him with us. He helped the owner carry out the dishes of food and clean up—we ate on the floor, sitting on pillows and using our hands most of the time. There were three or four of us staying in each of the rooms and instead of having the boy walk back in the freezing dark to the cliffs I had him sleep beside me on the floor. It was a simple, polite gesture. I was just trying to be a good Samaritan, but I knew it would create trouble for me one day. He stayed with me every night after that. Each night he slept closer and closer until we were sleeping together. It was just so natural. One day I knew I was in love with him."

"This was the fellow who drove the van?" I asked. "To the hospital. To Kabul?"

"Yes," Stan said. His body was tense, frozen into thought.

"How old was he?"

"I don't know."

Then again, after a pause, he added, "It was part of why I left. He was too young. I wasn't sure what I could give him. So I ran away."

"You ran away?"

"I left him in Kabul. I told him that I had to return to America for a while, because of a family problem; that I would be back soon. He took it okay, because I convinced him that I was coming back. There was no family problem."

"Are you going to go back?"

"I've gotten a new assignment. Working in India."

He lay still for a while, breathing slowly in and out. Then we both rose and showered together, stroking each other to another orgasm beneath the warm flow of water.

Clean, exhausted and back in the bed, I drifted off to sleep in his embrace. I sensed him stir hours later, rise out of bed and begin to get dressed. The activity roused Inky in the other room, and I groggily stayed awake until Stan was dressed and at the door.

"Good-bye and thanks," he said, as he left. "I hope you find him."

I nodded and closed the door, petting Inky and groping my way through the darkness of the apartment and back to sleep. I was by then too tired to miss him, but I knew I would in the days that followed.

W A Y N E L E E G A Y

Wayne Lee Gay completed the Ph.D. in Creative Writing at the University of North Texas, where he currently teaches in the English department. His fiction has appeared in *Swell, descant, SN Review,* and *Spilling Ink,* and his poetry in *New Millennium Writings* and in the anthology *The Weight of Addition.* He won first prize in the 2010 Saints and Sinners short story competition, the 2010 Frank O'Connor Award for Short Fiction from *descant,* and the 2011 David B. Saunders Award for Creative Nonfiction from *cream city review*. In an earlier career as a journalist, he was a finalist for the Pulitzer Prize for Criticism in 1990.

ONDINE

Wayne Lee Gay

Elizabeth wears her hair in a tight bun, a modest fashion, appropriate for a Christian girl. This is how her mother wears her hair, and this is how her father and their preacher, Brother Billy Thompson, want her to wear her hair.

But as she lifts her hands from the piano, and as the music ebbs away in the quiet living room, she has an urge to un-bind her hair, and let it flow loose down her back.

Sitting next to her, Dr. Bennett, her piano teacher, smiles, and says nothing.

Out in the yard, a young Mexican man looks up from his rake, and feels the last vibration of the music.

Ten miles away, in her office downtown, on the forty-fourth floor, Dr. Bennett's wife, Louise, looks out her window, across heat-scorched Dallas, toward the house and the pool. She shivers a little, and tells herself that the air conditioner is turned up too high.

"You've got the notes, dear," Dr. Bennett finally says, running his fingers through his thinning brown strands of hair. "But do you have any idea what the music is about?"

Twelve years ago, at the age of five, Elizabeth took her first piano lesson from Mrs. Bagby, a perfumed, efficient, and passionate woman who operates a successful piano studio in a neighborhood close to where Elizabeth and her parents live. Elizabeth proved to be the most amazing student in Mrs. Bagby's long career as a piano teacher; she read music effortlessly and memorized immediately. Within three weeks, she could play anything in the tattered hymnbooks at the storefront church she and her father and mother and little brothers attended. Elizabeth's father declared that she needed no more lessons, since, obviously, playing hymns was all she needed to do. Elizabeth overheard and spent the entire afternoon screaming with the inconsolable rage of a five year old, totally uncharacteristic in the strict fundamentalist household. Brother Billy Thompson, the preacher at their church, dropped in that evening on a pastoral visit, heard the child's distress, then listened to her play on the old upright piano Elizabeth's mother had inherited from her mother. He counseled Elizabeth's father that she had special gifts, and would doubtless be a witness for the Lord with her music.

Thanks to this advice from Brother Billy Thompson, a new, neat little spinet arrived in the Young family living room a few weeks later. Two years later, when the rapidly growing Church of the Holy Covenant of God moved from its storefront home to a beautiful new building, there was a nice grand piano in the sanctuary, on which Elizabeth played hymns and bits of the music from her lessons, and improvised combinations of the two, for an hour before morning worship service every Sunday.

On a cold, clear afternoon four years ago, eight years after her first lessons with Mrs. Bagby, thirteen-year-old Elizabeth and Elizabeth's mother and Mrs. Bagby drove from Mrs. Bagby's house to Dr. Bennett's house. Mrs. Bagby, highly respected as she was, suddenly found herself facing a student who far outstripped her own abilities. In spite of the cold, Elizabeth glistened with sweat as she played for Dr. Bennett, and wished she could loosen her tight bun of brown hair as she played Bach and Bartok, Chopin and Mozart and Schumann on one of Dr. Bennett's two grand pianos. Dr. Bennett, recognizing the rare talent that had walked into his living room, immediately asked—no, demanded—that Elizabeth appear for long weekly lessons at his house, or, sometimes, at his studio at the college where he taught.

"How much do you charge?" asked Elizabeth's mother, short and boxy in a plain brown dress, nervously fingering the large crucifix she always wore.

"Charge?" Dr. Bennett had replied, scratching his thinning brown hair, as if he didn't understand what she had said. "Oh, pay whatever you paid Florence," he said, nodding toward Mrs. Bagby.

"We'll have to ask Elizabeth's father," Elizabeth's mother said. "He is the head of our house, even as Christ is the head of the church. We'll pray about it."

Elizabeth, staring at the two large concert grand pianos in the room that overlooked the pool and the garden, felt sudden alarm and embarrassment. She knew it was time for her to move beyond Mrs. Bagby, and she yearned to play more on Dr. Bennett's pianos, both of which resonated with a sound even richer and more beautiful than the piano at Brother Billy Thompson's church.

"Could we start tomorrow?" Dr. Bennett asked, sensing that quick action was needed.

Feeling cornered, Elizabeth's mother neither agreed nor disagreed, but continued to finger her cross, nervously. Elizabeth longed more than ever to loosen her hair and let it flow down her back. As they left with Mrs. Bagby, Elizabeth's mother told Dr. Bennett that she would call him that night and let him know after talking to the head of their household. Elizabeth stared forward nervously all the way home, and Elizabeth's mother, suddenly feeling more sympathy for her daughter than fear of her husband, told her she could take the lessons, but should not mention to her father that she had a new teacher.

She forgot to call Dr. Bennett—what with all the fuss from her husband's return from a business trip. Dr. Bennett waited nervously at his house until three the next afternoon, and breathed a sigh of relief when he answered the doorbell and saw Elizabeth standing there, her scores gripped tightly to her chest.

~ ~ ~

For the next four years, Dr. Bennett resisted the temptation to push Elizabeth forward in contests, sensing that too much attention might wreck the delicate balance of church and family. She played occasionally for groups of his other students, some of whom were enrolled at the college, and some of whom were younger, and who came to him from the families of wealthy doctors and lawyers. Some of the students were jealous, some amazed—as were their mothers and fathers. Dr. Bennett occasionally invited Elizabeth to accompany him when he attended concerts with Louise; he gradually discovered that her mother would usually allow her to go if the all-powerful father and husband was away on a business trip, as he often was, but that she was not allowed to go if he was at home. Still, since Elizabeth and her two younger brothers were "home-schooled," staying up late on a school night was not much of a problem.

Elizabeth's father was, indeed, out of town on the early May night when Elizabeth rode to the concert hall and heard a French pianist, whose name Elizabeth could not pronounce. One piece in particular struck her as beautiful, as something she could imagine herself playing, as something, indeed, she could dream about at night. "I want to play *Ondine*," she announced to Dr. Bennett and Louise as they drove her home that night.

"That's pronounced 'ahn-dean,'" Louise said, smiling knowingly. Louise Bennett always smelled, Elizabeth had noticed, like the roses Elizabeth's mother tended in their garden at home; she always wore expensive, perfectly tailored suits, and she always complimented Elizabeth on her playing. But she always looked at Elizabeth as if there was something about her that she wasn't quite happy with.

"That's quite a challenge for a young pianist," Dr. Bennett had added.

"Have you ever played it?" Elizabeth asked.

He smiled, a little sadly, and said, "There was a time, dear, when I thought I could conquer the world with *Ondine*, and a few pieces like it."

Louise smiled, too. But at their next lesson, Dr. Bennett handed Elizabeth a copy of the music, in a set with two other pieces by Ravel, and gave her permission to start learning the notes.

Now, only a few weeks have passed, and Elizabeth knows the notes so perfectly she could probably write the piece out by hand if asked to. She plays every marking, following perfectly the instructions in the score for every forte and piano and accent and crescendo.

But the music is without life, Dr. Bennett thinks, scratching his head. How to explain to a seventeen-year-old girl, who doesn't even know any boys except her two younger brothers, about longing, and temptation, and love? Why, on Earth, he wonders, did God send such exceptional talent to the child of two willful, ignorant fundamentalists, who don't know Bach from Stravinsky, and don't care?

"Have you read the poem at the front of the score?" he asks. He runs his fingers through his hair, and Elizabeth smiles back at him, and shakes her head no.

"You see," he adds, "It's about a mermaid. Like in the movie. *The Little Mermaid*."

"We're not allowed to see Disney movies," Elizabeth explains, then mouths the explanation her parents have given her. "They are worldly, and they are the work of the devil."

She's suddenly conscious of how childish she sounds, at seventeen, and feels embarrassed and left out, just like when she explained to her cousin Marlene, when they were both twelve, that she didn't swim in pools with boys and men, and didn't watch television shows that other children watched, and didn't go to school, but stayed home and studied Christian math and Christian English and Christian science with her mother.

Dr. Bennett looks at her, and decides to risk an explanation.

"Well, you know what a mermaid is, don't you?" he asks, cautiously, remembering the irritatingly righteous mother, and imagining the tyrannical father he has never actually seen in person. "Ondine is a mermaid, and she wants to seduce"—he pauses, realizing he has chosen too strong a word. "She wants to lure men into the lake with her, so she can drown them, because, though she is very beautiful, she is also very evil."

He realizes why he has not bothered to explain the meaning of *Ondine* to Elizabeth already, and admits that he wanted her to learn the piece before she learned its erotic implications.

He opens his own score, on the piano in front of him, and begins to play, sounding very much like someone who once knew the piece very well but hasn't practiced it in a long time. In spite of the missed notes here and there, Elizabeth realizes that the tremolo is water in a lake, glistening in the moonlight, like the water in the pool, outside the big windows, glittering in the hot summer sun. And when the melody enters, she hears the wheedling and pining and longing of the seductive mermaid, and hears a little sadness and loneliness as well. And she thinks, maybe the mermaid is not entirely evil, but a little lonely, as well.

"She gets pleasure from tempting men into the water, and pulling them under the water, and feeding on their souls," Dr. Bennett says, managing to throw in a few words of explanation as he plays. But he doesn't even have to explain the part where Ondine becomes more desperate, as the music becomes louder, and rises, like waves. The music—and the mermaid—become angry, then sad, as Ondine finally gives up.

"Still, she laughs a little as she swims away," Dr. Bennett says.

The quiet ending makes Elizabeth a little sad, too. She decides, after Dr. Bennett is through, that she will think of *Ondine* a little differently. She decides to believe that the man has given in to the mermaid, and swims away with her, quietly allowing himself to drown, just to be with her, for just a moment, before he dies.

And then, Elizabeth realizes that if she can play the notes as perfectly as she already plays them, and make the music sound as full of longing and as wet and sad and cruel as it does when Dr. Bennett plays it, then the music will be truly beautiful. More beautiful than the lawn and the bright red flowers and the cool, blue swimming pool. Maybe even as beautiful as the handsome Mexican, who has now disappeared behind the tall green shrubs. She thinks about the music. And she looks out to where the young Mexican has disappeared behind the bushes, and begins to pretend that the music is about him. And then she pretends, hesitating, that the music is about herself.

Elizabeth decides that someday she will play for more than just the noisy people coming into the Church of the Holy Covenant of God on a Sunday morning. To the other people who hear her play it, the world and the cars and the televisions and the traffic will all disappear for a moment, and all that will exist and all that will matter will be the beautiful, cruel mermaid. And they will each, separately, each in his or her own mind, as if in a dream, leap into the water with the mermaid, giving themselves to her.

For the first time, she knows that the reason she wants more than anything in the world to play the piano is to know that people love her, and love her enough to give themselves to her for just a little while, and let her drown them in notes, and draw them away with her, so deep and far into the music they will disappear, if only for a little while.

Elizabeth knows she will not let her mother or father or Brother Billy Thompson know that the music is about a wicked, beautiful mermaid; that even on Sunday after church, when Brother Billy Thompson lingers a little, and smiles at her, if he asks her what the beautiful music is about, she will tell him that the splashy, beautiful music is about Jesus walking on the water.

Elizabeth listens attentively to Dr. Bennett's explanation of certain harmonic details in the music, but quits listening when the young Mexican comes out from behind the shrubs, wearing a tiny, tight black bathing suit. He is younger, much younger than Elizabeth's father or Dr. Bennett, but he is older than Elizabeth. His muscles are hard and golden in the sun; the tiny black bathing suit grips the middle part of his body. His hair is cut short like a soldier's.

When she sees the Mexican boy dive into the water, she wishes she could pull the pins out of her hair, and feel it flowing down her back, and dive into the water with him.

Dr. Bennett stares out at the swimming pool.

"I told Mundo he could swim in the pool after he gets done with the yard work," he explains, even though she hasn't asked.

~ ~ ~

After saying goodbye to Elizabeth, Dr. Bennett goes out to the pool to speak to Mundo, and to hand him the cash he owes him. Mundo knows that polite gringos, like Dr. Bennett, pay Mexicans like him in cash. To show him how much he appreciates it, Mundo bends and stretches and wipes himself with the towel a second time, lingering as he rubs his ankles completely dry, as if it is suddenly very important to be completely dry. Dr. Bennett watches him with a little smile, nervously scratching his head.

One of Mundo's roommates, Roberto, saves his money, and makes careful lists of groceries and supplies, so there's always something to eat at their apartment. He always sends part of his money home to his mother in Mexico.

But Mundo and Alex, his other roommate, spend all their extra money on dinners at cafés and restaurants, or on handsome silky shirts and cute pants at Ross. And, of course, on beers, or, if they're feeling rich, on shots of whiskey, at Miguel's, where they go to dance the salsa and the cumbia with the pretty Mexican girls—or at Starry Skies, where they go to hang out and dance with each other, or with the gringos who dress like cowboys and look at them with hungry eyes.

Now and then, Mundo and Alex buy a little weed from the slender, pretty black woman who lives in their apartment complex. When Mundo has weed, he shares with Alex, and when Alex has weed, he shares with Mundo.

Roberto owns the red truck they use to get to their yard work jobs, and to carry the mowers and weed eaters and bags of fertilizer. Sometimes Alex and Mundo beg Roberto to drive them down to Starry Skies or Miguel's, especially on a Friday or a Saturday night. At Miguel's, when Mundo dances the salsa with the pretty girls, he always watches to see which of the men are looking at the girl he's dancing with, and which are looking at him. At Starry Skies, he dances with Alex; while the twangy country-and-western music throbs around them, they always frown, at first, at the hungry-eyed gringos. Then, after a little while, they smile back and dance with them. Sometimes one or the other or both of them go home with one of the men for the night. And if one of the men looks like he might happen to want to help out with a little money, then Mundo and Alex are not above accepting. And sometimes they might even suggest that a little help with the rent might be a good thing.

Mundo wonders sometimes if he'll ever see Dr. Bennett at Starry Skies. Dr. Bennett always lets Mundo know when Mrs. Bennett will not be home until late, or when she has gone on a business trip, so Mundo can stay late and swim in the little black Speedo bathing suit he bought at Ross. Then, while the sun goes down, Dr. Bennett sits on the patio and drinks whiskey and watches Mundo swim, and offers him beer or Coca-Cola.

Mundo wishes Dr. Bennett would offer him whiskey. And he hopes that someday he'll ask him to come into his house, and play on the big piano, just for him. Mundo has never been inside the house, but he can see through the big windows, like a wall of glass overlooking the gardens and the swimming pool. He hears the beautiful music from the piano. He sees the kids come for lessons—the serious-looking, rich Anglo and Chinese and Japanese kids who play beautiful music.

Mundo wishes he could go inside the house, and touch the piano, and maybe even press down on the keys.

And if he did, he promises himself, he would go into the bedroom with Dr. Bennett, and do whatever Dr. Bennett wanted him to do. Alex had a friend, once, a rich gringo, not so very old, but not at all young, who gave him presents and took him on trips and gave him a gold chain to wear around his neck.

But Mundo doesn't want a gold chain.

Of all the kids who come for lessons, one is different, Mundo has noticed. He saw her today. She wears plain, dull clothes—brown dresses, and long-sleeved white blouses. She wears her hair tied up in a tight bun like a housemaid or a grandmother. When she plays the piano, it sounds like water flowing, and like rain in the forest.

Mundo would like to talk to her, and sit beside the piano while she plays. He would like to be her friend. Today, when she played, the music sounded like a waterfall, rushing around his arms and head like the water in the pool when he dived to the bottom and floated to the surface.

"My wife won't be home for a while, yet," Dr. Bennett says. "I need a little company. We could grill some steaks, like last week."

Mundo smiles, and takes the cell phone out of his jeans. He smiles at Dr. Bennett as he calls Roberto and tells him not to come until later, speaking in rapid Spanish.

Elizabeth has just opened the car door, when she remembers that she has forgotten one of her scores—the Bach. She runs back to the house, leaving her mother waiting, and rings the doorbell, and, when there's no answer, tries the door; it's unlocked. She dashes into the living room, sees the score on the floor beside the piano, and picks it up. As she turns, she glances out the back window. Mundo stands very close to Dr. Bennett, who smiles at Mundo, and strokes his chest, and fingers one of his nipples. Mundo smiles back, and touches Dr. Bennett's cheek with his hand. Elizabeth turns and walks slowly back to the front door, and down the sidewalk, to the car where her mother is waiting for her.

~ ~ ~

Brother Billy Thompson has told Elizabeth she can play whatever she wants on Sunday mornings, before church begins; she senses, however, that it's best to improvise on familiar old hymn melodies as more people arrive, as the start of the church service approaches.

This Sunday, an hour before church is supposed to start, she practices Schumann and Chopin and Bach, glad for a few minutes before she has to play the ugly hymns about blood and Jesus' love. The other teenagers go to Sunday School class; once, when Brother Thompson's wife, Sister Thompson, the teacher for the teenage class, asked why Elizabeth didn't come to the class, Brother Billy told her that the Lord had called her to play the piano. Sister Thompson, who had played the hymns herself on the tinny old upright at the old church, before Elizabeth learned to play the piano, had frowned a little, but kept quiet after that.

Sometimes, for Elizabeth, the music is like a building she walks through. Sometimes it's a country made of nothing but colors. Today, for a little while, she imagines fairies and angels dancing on the beams of light, or choirs singing in cathedrals with stained glass windows. She sees emperors and ballerinas. And mermaids.

She saves *Ondine* for last, just before she has to start playing the hymns. She thinks about Mundo and Dr. Bennett. She thinks about the beautiful, evil mermaid. She imagines Mundo and Dr. Bennett, swimming in the pool, naked. And in her daydream, she is with them in the pool, and she is naked, too.

To think of this is a sin, she knows, and she feels her cheeks turn red, and worries that someone may notice. She has not seen Dr. Bennett or Mundo swimming naked, but she saw something else at her last lesson that makes her able to imagine it, and even to imagine that she could be in the swimming pool with them.

The hymns are ugly, and make her feel sick, like eating too much candy. But she plays them, and is glad when she sees her mother, looking proud, sitting three rows back from the front, her hair tied up in a bun like Elizabeth's. It makes her almost ashamed to think how sad her mother would be if her mother knew what she was thinking.

She cares less about what her father would think if he knew. She used to care because he decided when she could have piano lessons and whether or not she could have a piano, but now Brother Billy has insisted that she must play the piano, and that it is God's work.

Elizabeth's father is stern as he tries to sing the hymns. And when the sermon begins, he listens carefully, and frowns, and nods in agreement with everything that Brother Billy Thompson says.

Elizabeth's brothers, Seth and Noah, two rows behind her parents, jab at each other and whisper and scribble notes. They're just quiet enough that their father won't hear and turn around and frown at them—or, worse yet, grab them by their collars and jerk them out the door of the church and slap them, as he has done before, so loud everyone in the church could hear.

Elizabeth is thankful Brother Billy Thompson wanted her to have a piano, even if he sometimes looks ridiculous in his red ties, while his Adam's apple bobs up and down and he gets madder and madder about secular humanists and evolutionists and abortionists.

Today, he preaches about Sodom and Gomorrah, destroyed by fire, and about evil men he calls *hormersexuals*. And he flips through his Bible frantically, almost tearing the pages as he finds one verse after another to prove his point.

Elizabeth has heard all of this before, and knows that it is really *homosexual*, not *hormersexual*. She found what it means in a book called *Questions and Answers for Christian Young People*: it means men who have sexual relationships with other men, the book said.

Brother Billy Thompson says that homosexuals—or, as he says, *hormersexuals*—lure young men into their evil ways. How else could more homosexuals come to be, since homosexuals cannot have children of their own?

At home, Mama and Seth and Noah and Elizabeth study Christian math and Christian literature and Christian biology. This explains how the world was made by God in seven days, and how this country was made by Christians who worshipped the one true God. And how God will destroy our country if we do not turn back to Him.

Last Wednesday, during her piano lesson, Dr. Bennett said that it was time for Elizabeth to think about auditioning to go to college at faraway schools called Curtis and Juilliard. Brother Billy Thompson wants her to go to a Christian college in Tennessee, where she will play the piano for good Christian young people, to the glory of God. Elizabeth's father says that girls don't need to go to college at all, and Elizabeth is not sure whether he really means it, or whether he might give in, like he did about the piano lessons and the piano.

The sermon is nearly over, and Elizabeth is hot, and wants to take the pins out of her hair. When she plays the last hymn after the sermon, she slips in secret bits of Chopin and Schumann that no one recognizes, and even a little bit of *Ondine*.

And she thinks another sinful thought, a very sinful secret, more sinful than the daydream of swimming naked with Mundo and Dr. Bennett.

~ ~ ~

By the time of her next lesson, Elizabeth has practiced *Ondine* so carefully that she can see the music in her mind—not so much as a piece of music, but as a house, in which she walks from room to room.

Today, just before she starts to play *Ondine* for Dr. Bennett, she remembers the sinful, secret thought she had last Sunday in church, more sinful than when she thought about being naked in the pool with Mundo and Dr. Bennett.

Today, she thinks about the evil mermaid as she plays. She thinks about a beautiful mermaid with long brown hair; hair like hers, only unpinned, unbound, free and flowing down her back. She imagines herself naked in the swimming pool, and she imagines Dr. Bennett and Mundo naked in the pool with her.

But that is not her most sinful secret thought.

Just as the music climbs and rushes upward to its most excited moment, she thinks about the time her worldly cousin Marlene spent the night with her, and how she touched her in places no else had ever touched her before.

But even that is not her most sinful secret thought.

As the music swirls away in that cold, beautiful, evil laughter at the end, she imagines Mundo holding Dr. Bennett under the water, and laughing, like Ondine. It is a horrible thought, she knows, but it makes the music sound more frightening and beautiful than before. And, horrible as that thought is, it is still not her most sinful thought.

The music ends. Dr. Bennett is crying as she turns and looks up at him, where he stands by the piano, running one hand through his hair.

"Elizabeth, dear, I think you've got it," he says.

Then, once again, Elizabeth thinks the most sinful, secret thought of all.

Dr. Bennett is quiet, for he sees that she is thinking. And he is right, though he does not know what she is thinking.

It is a thought she has thought before, though she has never before dared to form the words. And now, she forms the words, silently. She cannot stop herself.

And this is that sinful secret thought: that she loves this music more than she loves Jesus.

~ ~ ~

Mundo feels like he's inside a furnace. He drips huge beads of sweat as he pulls weeds from around the flowers, and then starts the lawn mower with a jerk of the cord. He will be glad when he can stop the mower, and swim in the pool, and hear the strange girl playing the beautiful music on the piano.

"Mrs. Bennett is out of town on business," Dr. Bennett said earlier, when Mundo arrived.

Mundo knows this means he can stay late, and swim in the evening, when the long shadows stretch across the pool and the lawn.

As he mows, he decides he will tell Dr. Bennett he has forgotten his bathing suit, and it won't matter, since there are not girls around, anyway, and the fence and hedge are so very high, no one can see over.

And Mundo hopes that Dr. Bennett will give him whiskey with his steak, and take him by the hand, and lead him to a bedroom, where there will be a big bed, with a thick, smooth blanket. And there will be beautiful paintings on the wall, and Mundo will do whatever Dr. Bennett likes, in the big, soft bed.

Mundo cuts the mower engine and pushes the mower toward the gate. He calls Roberto on his cell phone to tell him that he is done, but that he need not come to pick him up until tomorrow morning.

Roberto is silent and judging on the other end of the line. Mundo casually mentions how much Dr. Bennett will pay him in cash, so Roberto says, "Okay," and hangs up.

The yard is green, the flowers tall and red. The strange girl with her hair tied up in a bun is playing the piano. The music sounds like rushing water. Mundo slips behind the bushes, where no one will see, and strips off his jeans.

He stands naked under the sun for just a minute, and lets the music flow across his bare body. He stretches out on the grass behind the shrub, hidden from the world, and nearly falls asleep. When he nods awake, he senses that the music has been over for a long time. The girl is surely gone, he thinks, and he decides to step out from behind the shrubs, naked, and dive into the pool.

~ ~ ~

The front door opens. Dr. Bennett and Elizabeth are both a little startled when Louise Bennett comes into the living room.

"And how are you, Elizabeth?" she asks, staring at her as if she wishes she could change her in some way.

Louise explains that she has forgotten one of her bags for her business trip, and has stopped to pick it up on her way to the airport. Dr. Bennett sighs and smiles at her. Louise says that the mail has come, and that there's a letter from the Curtis Institute of Music.

"I think I know what this is," Dr. Bennett says, tearing the envelope open.

He peers down at the white paper as Louise walks back to her bedroom.

"Just as I thought," he says. "It's the auditions schedule for next year."

"Mama will pray about it," Elizabeth says.

Then she surprises herself, and surprises Dr. Bennett and Louise, who has returned to the living room, carrying a small valise.

"But I know that I will go to the audition, no matter what Daddy and Mama say."

She knows that her father will not like this at all, nor will Brother Billy Thompson. And she knows that her mother will pray and worry.

Dr. Bennett smiles, and Louise smiles, too.

"Can I give you a ride home, Elizabeth?" Louise says. "It's on the way to the airport."

Dr. Bennett looks relieved. Then they hear a splash as Mundo dives into the pool. They turn toward the tall windows, and see him, naked and brown and handsome, rushing to the bottom of the pool, then swimming to the surface, his golden, muscled arms wet and shiny.

"I—I told Mundo he could swim here when he got done with his work," Dr. Bennett explains, touching his hair nervously, though no one has asked.

"So I see," Louise says. Her eyes are wide at first, then turn into narrow slits as she looks at her husband.

Louise beckons Elizabeth to go ahead of her toward the door, then follows, then turns back for a moment.

"Have your fun, Kevin," Louise says to Dr. Bennett, her hand already on the doorknob. "Have your fun, but be careful. We'll talk when I come home. I've seen this coming, and I know what I want to do."

The air is heavy with the pleasant smell of swimming pools and mowed grass, mixed with the sour smell of the hot asphalt on the street, as Elizabeth walks toward the car. She looks toward downtown. It's so hot, the tall buildings look as if they are quivering in the heat. She can feel the heat of the sidewalk through her shoes as she walks.

When Louise starts the engine, a blast of cold from the air conditioner hits Elizabeth's face. She shivers a little.

Suddenly, her scalp hurts. The bun is appropriate for a Christian girl, she knows. And Brother Billy Thompson and her father tell her she must wear her hair that way. And her mother agrees.

But she doesn't want to wear her hair in a way that's appropriate for a Christian young woman anymore. She reaches up, and pulls the pins out of her hair and loosens the tight bun. Silky strands of shiny brown hair pour across her shoulders and down her back.

Louise Bennett looks at her and smiles. For once, Elizabeth thinks, she does not look as if she wants her to change.

Then Louise reaches in front of Elizabeth, and positions the sun visor so that Elizabeth can see herself in the mirror. She moves her hand to Elizabeth's head, and touches her hair for a just a moment.

"You know, Elizabeth, you're really very beautiful," she says, looking at her and smiling.

She imagines Elizabeth, just a little older, on a stage, sitting at a piano, with an orchestra. She imagines Elizabeth playing like thunder, as if she is praying to a strange, new god, and she strokes Elizabeth's hair rhythmically, in time with the imagined music. The picture in her mind is so beautiful, and Elizabeth is so beautiful, she wants to cry.

"And your hair," she says, "Your hair is so beautiful like this. You should always wear your hair like this."

ERNEST HARDY

Ernest Hardy is a Sundance Fellow whose film criticism and commentary have appeared in the *New York Times*, the *Village Voice*, *LA Weekly*, and *Millennium Film Journal*. As a music critic, he's written for *Rolling Stone*, the *Source*, *Vibe*, *Option*, the *LA Times*, the *LA Weekly* and *Request*, and was a contributor to the reference books *1,001 Movies You Must See Before You Die*, *Classic Material: The Hip-Hop Album Guide*, and *Hip-Hop: A Cultural Odyssey*. He co-edited the Lambda Literary Awards finalist *War Diaries* and is currently working on his third volume of cultural criticism, and a collection of poetry and short stories.

Cold and Wet, Tired You Bet...

Ernest Hardy

He gets so sad sometimes. Often, actually. It just wells up in him and breaks messily through the surface. Like in those science-fiction movies where the alien who's been hiding out in human form suddenly rips through its host body, shredding skin and cracking bones. Tentacles and strange limbs protruding from the places where back, legs and arms used to be. Poisonous saliva dripping from massive, double-set fangs that glisten. That's the way his sadness is. Except it's quiet. And it doesn't distort him so dramatically. If anything, it makes him smaller. He shrinks into it as it consumes him. He smiles (no fangs, no gnashing of teeth) and softly wills himself to disappear. He barely makes a sound.

"It's okay," he'll say, unable to look you in the eye. Smiling. "It's okay." His hands clench tightly and thrust deep into pants pockets, straining against the seams as his head bends slightly. He shrugs almost imperceptibly. "I'm cool."

I tremble when this happens. Like a terrified extra in a horror film. But I've learned not to make a sound. I've learned to swallow my own screams. Any reaction from me only twists his anguish, adds garnish of guilt to his psychic platter. My fear is that the transformation, as with the creature on the big screen, reveals the true being lurking beneath skin—in his case a man so possessed by his demons that they permanently own him. A man made small by history and memory and flight-not-fight reflexes that uncoil at phantom triggers. He believes he's going to hell.

Every kiss is resignation; every fuck is condemnation. He cannot take pleasure in his pleasure. He cannot find the joy in love. Cannot receive it and battles himself when he feels it. He's constantly at odds with his body and with mine. Late at night, I hold him while he flinches within the embrace. I whisper to him, "I would give you the world but I don't believe in the world. But I do believe in you."

He won't let himself feel joy because it fades, so he can't let himself trust it. Sadness and despair have been more faithful. They stay in place. They dig deep. You can turn your back on them and trust that they will still be there when you turn back around. Waiting. They hang around as long as you feed them and they don't need much to flourish. He hasn't yet learned that joy has to be fed too. It's not self-sustaining. You have to clear a place for it. Make it feel welcome. Let it know that you want it. He hasn't learned that while sadness might seem to subsist solely on cigarettes and coffee, it's constantly snacking behind his back, cleaning out pantry and fridge. It's voracious.

We often lie in this fashion in bed at night: I am on my side, facing him. He lies on his back. One of my arms is folded beneath my head while the other safety-belts across his chest. I throw a protective thigh over his thigh. He rests his head on a pillow that is so old, so flat and limp, that it's folded twice to give it heft. His eyes are cast downward, looking absently at his chest and stomach. His arms are akimbo, angled slightly so that each hand nervously flutters a fingertip tap dance on his lower belly. I stroke his chest. He swallows nervously. We've been together well over a year now and he still has an ingénue's stage fright. No, he has the terror of someone stranded in a completely foreign land sans map or knowledge of the culture or native language. Just before he falls asleep, he turns to his side and softly slides back against me, his bare ass against my hard-on. I kiss his shoulder, buckling arm and thigh around him.

How it works: You draw up a list of what you want, what you need. Then from that master list you subhead items that you absolutely must have, things on which you will not compromise. And then you meet someone and fall in love and the list is thrown out a window.

This is the part you may not understand. I lean on him. On the Germanic sturdiness of his insecurities and fears; they're constants in our days, act as guideposts through our nights. They're dependable guardrails. I want to dismantle them so that he—so that we—can be free, but I'm nervous about what that freedom might mean, what might lie beyond it. Will he need me then? Who will he be? And have I come to romanticize the very thing from which I claim to want to free him?

My body can't contain its history. It gives everything away. In repose I sit slightly hunched forward due to hereditary scoliosis. I cannot bend my right arm properly because I broke it when I was a child; it was set badly but we were too poor to get it corrected after it had healed. When I get flustered I stutter, my eyes blink rapidly and I swallow after every word—hair-trigger heirlooms from constant confrontations with a father embittered because he'd sired a faggot, and he missed no chance to hector, belittle and voice his disgust. Faint scars line my left wrist: Sixteen, without hope, unable to see a future. Death wasn't really the goal but it was an acceptable risk for the reprieve sought. Molecular memory of my own distress is the root of my empathy for him. My man.

We speak the language of romance novels and five-hankie weepies with utmost sincerity.

"If I save you, will you save me?" I ask him with a smile, sans irony but with ulterior motive. His ego is fragile. I geisha myself three feet behind him to make him feel strong, to mask the strenuous work required to nurture and carry him. He knows but if he knew it would shatter him. And sometimes I coast on the surface of my whispered nocturnal queries, staying above subtext or flipped meaning, letting the words that are spoken do all the heavy lifting. I volley the role of hero into his court. To be truthful, sometimes I do want to be the imperiled Pauline yanked from the rails with only seconds to spare before the steam engine crushes me, confident that the cavalry is on its way and that my life is worth Herculean effort. That it's worth saving. Trembling, endangered captive is a cakewalk compared to twenty-four-hour savior.

"I don't know," he smiles back. "All the magazines and Oprah say you gotta save yourself." (*Sans irony*.)

"Fuck Oprah. I don't give a fuck about myself. I really don't. I don't care if I live or die except for you. I get it up for you. I would do anything to take care of you, to make you feel safe. Would you do the same for me?"

He thinks a long time. I wait. "Okay," he says finally. "I'll take care of you. I'll protect you." He grins sheepishly.

Robert Glück is the author of nine books of poetry and fiction, including two novels, *Margery Kempe* and *Jack the Modernist* and a book of stories, *Denny Smith*. Gluck edited, along with Camille Roy, Mary Berger and Gail Scott, the anthology *Biting The Error: Writers on Narrative*. Glück was Co-Director of Small Press Traffic Literary Arts Center, Director of The Poetry Center at San Francisco State, and Associate Editor at Lapis Press. His poetry and fiction have been published in the *New Directions Anthology, City Lights Anthologies, Best New Gay Fiction 1988* and *1996, The Norton Anthology of World Literature, Best American Erotica 1996* and *2005*, and *The Faber Book of Gay Short Fiction*. His critical articles appeared in *artforum international, Aperture, Poetics Journal,* and *Aufgabe,* and he prefaced *Between Life and Death*, a book on the paintings of Frank Moore.

ROBERT GLÜCK

The Devil is a Woman

(from *About Ed*)

Robert Glück

The Devil is a Woman was part of a Josef von Sternberg retrospective in 1973 at a theater in the Castro that has long since disappeared.

From the internet: Adapted from the same Pierre Loüys novel that spawned Luis Bunel's *That Obscure Object of Desire, The Devil is a Woman* (1935) is set in an intricately conceived studio version of Spain that situated Marlene Deitrich in the middle of a love triangle with an older military man and a young revolutionary. Both suffer the exquisite agony of being snubbed by her. The beautiful and the arbitrary reign together in the form of Concha Perez, a cigarette factory worker, who tells one of her admirers, "If you really loved me, you would have killed yourself." *Devil* is a fascinating farrago of decadent romanticism, 30's left-wing activism, and Sternberg's preoccupation with authoritarianism and freedom.

Josef von Sternberg and his discovery, Marlene Dietrich, worked together for the last time on this notorious box-office flop. Antonio Galvan (Cesar Romero), a young military officer, meets alluring Concha Perez and soon falls under her spell. Antonio confesses his love for Concha to his friend Don Pasqual (Lionel Atwill), an older and higher-ranking officer. Pasqual is horrified when he learns of Antonio's infatuation; years ago, he and Concha started a long, disastrous relationship in which she repeatedly lured him into her web and drained him of his wealth. The film was thought to be lost until Dietrich provided a print from her personal collection for a Sternberg retrospective in 1959. John Dos Passos co-authored the screenplay.

CONCHA: Arturo, a cup of coffee.

PASQUAL: My emotions seem to make little impression on you. Aren't you afraid of anything, Concha? Have you no fear of death?

CONCHA: No, not today. Why do you ask? Are you going to kill me?

PASQUAL: You play with me as if I were a fool. What I gave gladly, you took like a thief.

CONCHA: I thought you would be glad to see me. I'm sorry I sat down.

The Devil is a Woman was the most controversial movie of the 1930's. The Spanish government demanded that Paramount pull the motion picture out of circulation and destroy all copies of the film. Paramount only withdrew the movie when the U.S. State Department asked them to do so. The movie lost heavily at the box office and the careers of Marlene Dietrich and the other cast members as well as many of the production crew were irrevocably damaged.

During the years 1930-1935, the single most successful tandem in Hollywood was that of Sternberg and Dietrich. Sternberg did the photography himself and Dietrich comes across as an evil goddess, her beauty on the edge of absurdity. This film was Dietrich's all time favorite.

CONCHA: What did you do?

ANTONIO: Politics. A little bit revolutionary.

CONCHA: Is that all? I thought it was something important.

I have no trouble crying, but I need this story because of its glycerin tears. I cry very easily, all I have to do is begin making the motions and in a minute I am crying deeply. Possibly I am depressed—but more often I have the pre-tears feeling that comes after reading a long Russian novel. How impossible to contain, as one must, all the time that has passed, generations, and the characters, their childhoods, adulthoods, and deaths. The great events of history and the arbitrary ways they impinge on the individual and all the possible outcomes and reversals at every moment in the story which gather to make an emptiness of potential that rides along the story inside each breath, a vast emptiness that incriminates each breath. That's why I associate these tears, which seem to contain so much distance, with the experience of aging. It is the expression of intolerable distance, distance impossible to contain, so while I may be congested with feeling and suffering and my body clenched and even wracked, there is also a delicate filigree, a pattern mostly empty, which I enjoy with a kind of recognition, the spatial equivalent of a death's head, but lovely, or rather, harder to endure. It is often said that people who age best live in the moment, or even that one lives in the moment as one ages whether intending to or not, so maybe as I grow older any awareness of larger amounts of time equals mourning.

PASQUAL: I love you, Concha. Life without you means nothing.

CONCHA: One moment and I'll give you a kiss.

In particular I cry after movies, not so much in the theater, but at home at my dining room table, even over dessert. Any movie really. I associate this with my aging because movies compress so much time, and I wonder if I am more "in touch" with my feelings, as we used to say. We used to say, "We've got to get ourselves together," and nothing seems more improbable, since we never got ourselves together and we are less likely to do so now. "I've got to get myself together"—nothing is less likely. How will Ed, who is no longer alive, get himself together? In that era, the early seventies, we went to movies that supported an overall sexuality and an aesthetic position that repressed the difference between figure and ground. I am thinking of the duel scene in *The Devil is a Woman*. It was part of a Sternberg retrospective in 1973 at a theater on 18th Street in the Castro in San Francisco that has long since disappeared.

Pasqual has never been able to cure himself of his addiction to Concha, and when he encounters Concha with Antonio at a street festival, Pasqual is overcome with jealousy and challenges Antonio to a duel. The duel takes place in a forest at dawn. Dietrich wears black lace as though already mourning the death that she has instigated. She raises a black lace parasol. This is what Ed and I took from the film: In order to make the screen dazzle, Sternberg slid beads of glycerin down hundreds or thousands of invisible strings, slow rain, each drop catching its portion of light and carrying it downward.

The roar of rain out of proportion to the slow movement of light, just as the roar of sex is out of proportion to Dietrich's indifference, or to the act of penetration, an imbalance that gave her a fairy tale passivity.

It is hard to write about that image without reverting to somber camp—to wear myrtle in my butthole. It was camp ten minutes after it hit the screen in 1935. What did it mean to fabricate such an elaborate spectacle for the act of penetration? To support it with so much beauty. To subvert it with so much melodrama. To support it with so much artifice. To elaborate the pure and impure, saint and whore, love of flesh and horror of flesh, the perpetual dualism of hips pumping.

CONCHA: Ha! This is superb. He threatens me. What right have you to tell me what to do? Are you my father? No! Are you my husband? No! Are you my lover? Well I must say you're content with very little.

Languid descent, slow beauty that Ed and I imported into our slow hippie lives, slow and anxious, as though Sternberg were directing Ed and me. That is, slow from arousal, slow from fear, arousal never completely expelled, fear never meeting its source in consummation.

I don't think we understood the deep mourning of this image, we could not add that to our mix of decadent romanticism and counter-culture politics. Obsession was always my subject. Ed, living or dead, a brick wall to beat my head against. What for?—to distract myself from the knowledge of death.

The acting in the film is no better than a PTA skit. Dietrich is supposed to be alluring but she has only one note: swagger. She's almost macho, as though she were besting the men with her cunt. But it is her sheer indifference that sets her apart, as though she were indifferent to the costume drama on every level. Her indifference is the story Sternberg tells: Dietrich's indifference to him, her indifference to the other actors, to the script, to her immediate fate, but not to the lighting man or to the light.

Not sex, but light—which Ed painted his way towards: the naked men floating towards the edge of the canvas and then away—leaving clouds, sky and light, experiments in empty space and arousal. That is what the glistening drops meant to us. They were light and they were tears. Not tears for the death in the film, those cardboard cut-outs were never alive, but tears shed by the oracle as she blathers nonsense that must be interpreted: something bad is going happen. Something bad is coming our way.

Yes it is an oracle of some kind. Align yourself with light and the knowledge of death, thank the camera man, the lighting man, make sure they are on your side.

What was our confusion?—her make-up was grotesque, the white skull dome, the pencil eyebrows in perpetual surprise, the jaw hollow at the corners. Like a Mario Bava witch, an Argento witch. Whatever protected the inside of her body against itself has vanished, the tendons snap over bone, the pain flares from her wrists and knuckles.

A few nights ago I had this dream: Hitler appears and I say to my friends, Hey, there's Hitler, let's kill him. They say, Oh yeah, Hitler, he's looking good. Hey guys, I say, it's Hitler, comm'on, we've got to kill him. They say, He's in good shape these days—yah, he looks OK. I was Bob and what does Bob know about killing someone? Hey guys, let's kill Hitler. Besides, the worst already happened so what was the point? That was Dietrich's stance too, that was the Weimar expression: the worst already happened. I picked up a rock and threw it at Hitler, but it landed a few feet away from me. He wasn't even upset. That's what the skull face of Dietrich was saying, that the worst already happened—that's why we could not understand or interpret her at the time—the early seventies—the worst had not yet happened. That's what her passivity was based on, her indifference, bringing that news of mourning into the realm of the sexual which, it seemed to us, was founded on hope and possibility. Obsession, which is the fear of death, obsessive love, erotic mourning. The skull was already laughing through the pinched starving face, the enlarged eyes.

CONCHA: Good morning. Good morning! Good morning! Good morning! I came to see if you were dead. If you had loved me enough you would have killed yourself last night. Bad. Not made properly. I can make much better chocolate.

Instead of commanding you to live, your lover commands you to die. She takes a lively interest in your death, since she is dead. You are left with nothing to grasp, nothing to believe, nothing to understand. Oh Ed, can I find my way to you on the back of this fucked-up image, the lacy black parasol, the glycerin tears sliding down a thousand strings? As though my goal is to find you?—to make our love last forever?—to add images to the endless images in the world? You have been gone for fifteen years and I will die before too long. It is something like love and something like revenge to put experience into words: my unrequited love for the world.

(I break a promise to myself—I promised that I would not speak to Ed in the second person, as though language could float me "over" to where he is. A promise more than an aesthetic decision. I am talking to his photo or his image in my mind. Not the Ed I saw last, but younger. Am I mourning my lack of access to his beauty—the glory of my own youth, arousal and glycerin tears—or his death which took place twenty-five years later? My feelings are hemmed in by the reversibility of childhood and set free by the irreversibility of death. Is that true? Sometimes I say Oh Ed. If I could "unpack" that sigh it would cover this book and a lot more. Maybe there's a way of talking to Ed that I am not prepared to do in public. I'll make myself naked when company comes, but I am reluctant to talk to Ed in your presence. And how does a dead person speak?—In a voiceover, from the future, about events leading to his death.)

"It Takes All Kinds" is excerpted from **Michael Alenyikov**'s first book, *Ivan and Misha,* winner of the 2011 Northern California Book Award for Fiction (as well as nominated for the Publishing Triangle's Edmund White Award for Debut Fiction). His short stories have appeared in Canada's *Descant, The Georgia Review, The James White Review, New York Stories,* and *Modern Words* in addition to appearing in *Best Gay Stories 2008.* He has written for *The Gay & Lesbian Review;* he was a MacDowell Fellow; and was nominated for a Pushcart Prize. Alenyikov has worked as a bookstore clerk, clinical psychologist, cab driver, and freelance writer. While a native of New York City, he currently lives in San Francisco.

MICHAEL ALENYIKOV

It Takes All Kinds

Michael Alenyikov

They never got naked, so Smith figured it didn't count as cheating. It was a hands-into-unzipped-pants, shirts-unbuttoned kind of business and the other guy—a Danny or a Tony, Smith wasn't all ears when he'd said his name—called him dude in a husky voice, which was a turn-on the first time, but by the fourth or fifth time after he'd guided Smith onto the leather couch in his apartment, it was a major *turnoff* and thus something of a relief.

Okay, they had kissed, which was a turn-on. His touch was rough, quick, searching, and yes, it was new, *unpredictable,* but just as Smith began to lose himself he thought of Misha: Misha's unhurried ways, his whispering "I love you" before they came. How Misha played Smith's body like a sax or an oboe, his instinct for shifting intensity and tempo with tender talk in English and Russian before they came together. How did he pull off that trick? No American-born man could make love like this. Smith, whose experience had been limited to boys from Michigan, had concluded it was a gift, ancestral magic passed on from one generation to the next, known only to men from frigid, faraway Russia.

Misha had a soul—*dusha* in Russian—and Smith wished he could steal it and make it his own.

Staring into Danny's or Tony's vacant eyes (he'd given up on Smith and was trying single-mindedly to get himself off), Smith thought of Misha's sad blue eyes waiting for him just three blocks away. The pain in them, were he to find out. They had rarely fought in their two years together. Skirmishes, of course, but quickly repaired. Misha's too-present brother, Ivan, was often the cause, until Smith learned that if he wanted—and he'd come to crave—Misha's near-mystical way with love, an unbounded affection for family was the price.

Smith's sense of family was American, prickly, unsettled. "Mish, I have very ambivalent feelings toward my family," he'd explained. "There's no word in Russian for ambivalence," Misha had said. Smith doubted this. And the truth is that he missed his family, especially his sister, Joanne. When Jo had visited last year, Misha said, "She is wonderful. Explain your silly ambivalence to me." Then Misha, poking a finger into Smith's chest, had declared, "Smitty, it is time to give up childish nonsense."

Now, Smith buttoned his shirt, zipped his pants. He scooped up his bag of groceries—the tomatoes and red peppers, the pale green lettuce wilting in the summer heat, the ice cream melting—and cast a backward glance at the dude-guy, whose muscles were tensed, his face contorted and sweaty. He looked like a laborer at day's end lifting one last pile of bricks, not at all like a man reaching for ecstasy.

"You can't go now," he said.

"Sure can," said Smith, halfway to the front door.

"It's rude, man, really rude."

"It takes all kinds," said Smith, closing the door quietly behind him.

Smith hated to fight. And he hated to cheat. But he had worries and this Tony or Danny with his lean body and muscle T-shirt seemed a solution of sorts. Spotting him at the Korean's on Avenue A, Smith, who'd been tapping cantaloupes for ripeness, had followed him into the Odessa, taking the open seat next to him at the counter. Before Smith could order an iced coffee, the stranger said smoothly, "Come see my paintings," stroking Smith's arm, after barely a nod and a hello. "I live upstairs."

Smith now raced down those stairs and stopped. He had three blocks to collect his thoughts. He'd been faithful to Misha for two long years—eight seasons in all! How could he be so stupid? *Come see my paintings.* Such a pathetic cliché; Smith blushed at the memory. And what if Misha found out? He could blame Ivan for taking up too much of Misha's time. But that was old news. I've never sown my wild oats, he thought, trying out that old line. But it too was another cliché. He was turning twenty-one next month. That had more potential. It was substantial, a birthday of consequence. A time for reflection, decision. I won't be young anymore, he thought, reaching for the right note of vindication. But the sound he heard was the errant clank of a child at the piano. More to the point, their anniversary was Labor Day, just one week away, and Smith was learning to say, to pronounce properly, I love you—*Ya tebia liubliu*—in Russian, as his gift. It had proved harder than he'd expected. Ivan was an impatient tutor, no substitute for Louie, Mish and Ivan's father. (How Smith's heart ached at the memory of the old man!) And often, of late, he didn't know if it was true, this sentiment: this I, Smith, loving you, Misha. And sometimes it was so true it frightened him.

Smith took the long way around Tompkins Square Park. The sun was hot, but cooled with each passing cloud, fall's chill fingering its way through the late August heat. He looked up, squinting at the sun. Was love so important in the greater scheme? Was it not more than a little self-indulgent? There was the thinning of the ozone layer, after all, and the melting of the polar ice caps, about which Misha had said, "Who cares, Smitty?" One year into the new millennium complacency reigned. At times, Smith believed he could see the earth's atmosphere escaping into the emptiness of space, the vacuum of the cosmos sucking him up with all those he loved. He'd bought a ticket to Antarctica, an excursion with Greenpeace. He'd not told Mish, not sure why until this very moment, clutching the bag of groceries tight to his chest: he might not come back—to school, to New York, to Misha.

And now Jo was about to visit. A whirlwind trip, she said, to see my only brother. She avoided discussing her engagement: his Jo planned to marry a dentist! Only he could save her from this foolishness but he had so much on his mind and though he loved her dearly he'd not found the courage to say, "Not a good time for a visit, Sis."

All reasons enough for a slip up on Smith's part.

He had a way of analyzing problems that was half his own and half his mother's influence. It hadn't been easy having a psychologist for a mom in Ann Arbor. She analyzed everything. She'd probably know exactly why he'd told Mish he was from Michigan's Upper Peninsula, why he'd lied about something so small.

The language stuck in his head: low self-esteem, projection, transference, the strengths and weaknesses of the ego, the power of the unconscious. Plus it had humiliated him when she took up with a graduate student half her age: Henry, a student in his father's department. Henry was skinny, still had zits, and sprouted pathetic patches of fuzz on his boyish cheeks. He called her Mrs. Doddsworth when he first came to the house for a meeting with his father. Soon she became Helen (a name she'd later spurn for Helena), then sweetheart. Henry breezed into the Doddsworth split-level like it was his, lengthening his spine so his head—in his dreams!—was positioned for a crown. Who did he think he was, master of the house? It made Smith sick.

She was the cheat! And when he learned that his father, Charles Doddsworth, professor of mathematics, had his own half-his-age mistress—at the same time!—who called him Chuck, he was crushed. Jo, older, trying on blasé for size, said, "Everyone's parents do it, why not ours?"

That's when Smith, born Robert (Robbie) Doddsworth, first changed his name.

If they could change, so could he. He waved hello to Z-man, a runaway street kid, a twig of a boy, who sold weed and kept Smith abreast of the latest happenings; to Sue-Ellen, pushing a stroller, hugely pregnant since he'd last seen her, who'd sighed about giving up her law job and treated Smith as if he were her only confidant; and to the quartet of old men playing chess in the shade, who still insisted they were from Yugoslavia. He felt he belonged in this teeming postage-stamp-sized neighborhood, this East Village, as he'd never felt he belonged in Ann Arbor.

He'd called himself Lawrence for a while. He'd seen *Lawrence of Arabia* at the campus theater and been mesmerized: sand, flowing white robes, desert dust storms, camel caravans, Peter O'Toole's bare chest.

Death too young on a motorcycle was very cool. No one got the reference, of course. Jo did with some explaining, but wasn't impressed. His mom said, "You're my Robbie. Whatever you do, I love you." She suggested he play his music louder as therapy when he lamented losing his dad. "Robbie, he's not exactly lost," she said. "He's five miles away."

Then the diagnosis. His mom was dying. The end came quickly. At the funeral he called himself Zero. His dad, distraught, confused, asked tersely, "Zorro? Are you calling yourself Zorro now? Robbie, it's Mom's funeral. It's time to grow up, son."

He'd never called him *son* before.

"No, Dad," he'd said, as a gentle drizzle fell over the large gathering. "My name is Zero."

Smith's father was tall, wide in the shoulders, and leaned over so often to hear people talk that there was a permanent curve to his spine. As the rain grew heavy, he opened an umbrella and tilted it to cover his son. Smith often replayed the scene in his head, like a movie whose meaning shifted on repeated viewings; it made him dizzy how quickly memory created a father at his mother's grave who spun from strong, to lost, to bitter.

He stopped. Something was wrong with his memory. He struggled to recall what was missing. Jo! Why wasn't Jo at the funeral? He did remember that everyone took his new name, Zero, to be a worrisome sign: "low self-esteem, unresolved grief . . ." The obvious was missed in Ann Arbor's culture of self-analysis: the mathematics of zero, the jargon of Dad.

He was paying homage.

"Yo, Smitty," the super's son, Julio, greeted him, wakening Smith to the heat, the groceries, and… Damn! He'd forgotten to buy the liter bottles of Diet Sprite Misha loved.

"Hey, what's happening?"

"You know, everything, nothing." Julio, pants below his waist, backward baseball cap and down jacket in the summer, looked the part of a drug dealer. But he was his father's eyes and ears, keeping the street safe—a dying breed in this gentrified neighborhood. Smith had seen a touring company perform *Rent* in Ann Arbor a dozen times and ached for the bad, good old days he'd missed when the neighborhood had an edge, a soul—when, legend had it, art and danger combined to transform life into an elixir to be drunk with abandon, or so he imagined.

He jiggled the key to the lobby. His was the second set of Misha's original. Ivan had the first, but Smith still thought a second copy gave him distinction. He knew little of Misha's old boyfriends, although he'd once overheard Misha and Ivan in a heated argument, whispering *Kevin, Kevin* as if the name were a tennis ball smacked from one brother to the other, Ivan's tone bitter, Misha's chagrined.

Afterwards, he'd asked. "An old boyfriend," Mish said, yawning, rubbing his eyes, as if he'd been questioned about the weather. "Do not concern yourself, Smitty."

This was another worry: was he good for Misha? How could he know if he didn't know Misha before they'd met?

"Do I make you sad?" he'd once asked when Misha's expression turned inward, and Misha smiled. "I am from Russia. We are born to be sad."

If Smith understood human nature at all, it ended at Misha. Mish was the unknown. Smith wanted a time machine. He wanted a snapshot from the past, home movies. Louie had known, but it was a parent's knowing, and Louie was almost one year dead. Do a thousand *I love you's* from Misha keep their meaning forever?

The hallway smelled of cat piss—the old Puerto Rican lady on the first floor or as easily the old Polish man, her neighbor. They hated each other. You'd think at their age they'd have something in common, reasons to be friends, but *people don't act sensibly* was one of the few rules in life Smith had learned that stood the test of time. Misha's loving him, for example, was not sensible. And labeling his own feelings low self-esteem did not help with this puzzle.

When Smith left for New York, Charles, or rather Chuck, drove him to the airport in his yellow sporty Mazda. Breaking long silences, he'd said, "Keep in touch, Robbie," and "I'm up to be departmental chair soon," and "Call collect." Smith didn't remember in which order. The word *love* floated unspoken in the tight confines of the car. Politely, Smith said, "Sure," "Great," and, "Call collect? Dad, that's so last century." He felt unforgiving. Chuck never knew how to say what was in his heart. Smith had promised himself that he'd not make this mistake. At the airport, his father wrapped his arms around him; it had the awkward sense of discovery, as if this were the first hug ever between two people, a grand revelation akin to solving a mathematical puzzle, Fermat's last theorem, perhaps, that had resisted the best minds over the centuries.

Smith now raced up the stairs, two at a time, ravenous for Misha.

"Mish," he croaked, his voice strangled by panic and guilt. What if he carried the dude-guy's smell on his body? He wanted to dive into bed with Mish, vaporize the recent past—the little cheating business (he'd reduced it to that) and a long string of pasts back to snowy Michigan Sundays, when he was Robbie Doddsworth and Robbie would burst into his parents' room and snuggle the morning away in bed with them.

"Hold it a minute, Smitty," Misha said. "I'm on with Ivan. Some kind of trouble." Smith dropped the groceries just loud enough to suggest annoyance. "Oh, and Jo called. Your Mom's coming, too."

Smith sighed. The funeral scene had been so comforting. The fantasy of his mother's dying was not new, but never so real. It had taken away the shame of what he'd just done. But the goodbye from Chuck was painfully true. He put the groceries away, half listening to Misha chatter in English and Russian.

~ ~ ~

At work the next day, Smith was relieved to be chopping onions. He'd spent the evening preparing potatoes for the latkes—the restaurant's claim to fame—although he preferred the pierogis and blintzes. Shredding those stubborn potatoes was an uncreative chore. But onions! He'd mastered dicing them to the edge between being and nothingness his father might appreciate. Besides, they made him cry. He needed a good cry, even if dicing onions was an artificial means to that end.

Smith had been worrying about the rain forests when Uli, his boss, switched him to onions. Uli was German, a barrel-chested brick wall of a man. Smith had been hired thanks to a brief conversation—in German—between Ivan and Uli. Ivan drove a cab. He was smart enough to do better, but didn't seem to care. "I like meeting people. What's the crime in that?" he'd say to Misha when the brothers quarreled—more often since their father's death. Smith wanted to learn Russian. He wanted to speak to the brothers on their own terms. He still knew so little and was especially confounded by their way with consonants: the unnatural acts with his tongue that Ivan insisted were required and which made Smith sound like he was lisping.

But the poor rain forests. They were disappearing. He'd read about it in *Time, Mother Jones,* and *Scientific American.* There were urgent warnings in *National Geographic* and *Nature. Nova* reported the consequences in somber terms; literature from Greenpeace was his bedside reading. A documentary etched forever in his mind the huge swaths of forest and jungle cleared for profit. But culpability was confused. The indigenous peoples were both victims and perpetrators. Smith preferred good and evil more clearly defined. He did not like this unfamiliar territory where right and wrong were muddled.

He'd been deeply troubled, outraged!...by a map illustrating how New Orleans, Bangladesh, Amsterdam, the many islands of Japan, Indonesia, the Philippines—and Manila, poor Manila!—would vanish beneath rising seas.

When his cell phone chirped, his hand slipped and he cut his index finger.

"Fuck it," he muttered. He grabbed a clean towel and wrapped his finger, listening to Joanne, irritated by her Michigan accent, so apparent to him now after two years in New York.

"No, not you, Sis," he said.

"Robbie, what's wrong? Is everything okay?"

"Yes. No. Hey, bad time."

"Robbie, getting married isn't the end of the world."

"To a dweeb it is. Have you lost your mind?"

"Then let's talk about where Mom and I will stay. Like, you know, you little twit, to make *p-l-a-n-s*." Smith pretended to hate it when Joanne spelled out words, but the truth was it made him feel protected, that she was still watching out for him. "Stop avoiding me," she said.

"I repeat. Can't talk and *p-l-e-a-s-e* get the *n-a-m-e* right. It's not Robbie and you're a twit for bringing Helena. So, so, so…" Smith was stutteringly mad: "bye-bye, ciao-ciao, do-do svidanya." *Good-bye* was the one expression he could say in Russian!

He'd adored Jo for as long as he could remember. "You are in my thrall," she'd say when they were young, in the voice of a stage hypnotist, subtly mocking Helena's therapy voice, wiggling her fingers in front of his eyes. They were each other's confidants. He was Robbie then. Helena was Helen, Chuck was Charles, and they were a family. Jo and Robbie were raised to amount to something. They were assumed to have prodigious talents in keeping with their parents'. Helen Doddsworth (born Smyth, she was one-quarter Welsh) had regretted taking her husband's name. She'd had brains, looks, and ambition but had given in to an archaic romantic fantasy. When Jo was born, she put off graduate school to be a stay-at-home mother. None of her girlfriends had proven so weak. To what syndrome had she succumbed? One day—with Joanne a toddler and Smith just learning to crawl—sick to death of diapers and baby talk, she'd bought seventy loaves of bread. (Seventy had a biblical ring to it, she thought.) They littered the kitchen floor, spilling over into the dining room. When Charles came home he'd raised a questioning eyebrow. "Asshole!" she screamed, throwing loaves at him. "I won them. I can be a breadwinner too, damn you."

"Bread pudding for dessert, sweetheart?" Charles had said, retreating to his study.

She returned to school, earned a Ph.D. in record time, and became a psychotherapist; she wanted to help others strip away their romantic fantasies and see the world as it was.

Helen had been an English major and named Jo for the Jo in *Little Women* and Robbie for *Robinson Crusoe,* markers to remind them to be independent, inventive. Their names sat in the unconscious of Jo and Robbie like pacemakers, reminding their weak-willed hearts to beat with ambition.

When Jo showed an affinity for math, Charles took a fatherly interest in her for the first time; he smiled with delight whenever she spoke. Charles Doddsworth was establishing a major minor career in the world of mathematics. An article, "Parsing Infinity: The Cosmos and Its Kin," had caused quite a stir and not a little celebrity. He became a popularizer, settling for book tours in place of discoveries in the realm of higher mathematics.

Robbie was a good listener, with a gift for empathy, Helen noted. Helen acted pleased that he and Jo were not conforming to gender stereotypes, although secretly she was uneasy. But she believed in working with what was at hand and not with what-if's. She taught Robbie that problems in life have causes that can to some extent be understood, and from understanding will come insight and action. He began to nod thoughtfully when listening to others. He took to saying "to some extent" precociously.

Jo, older by two years, grew disenchanted first. In high school, her quest to understand the mathematics of infinity was postponed when her body matured. In quick succession, she slept with a boy in the senior class, her high school math teacher, a student of her father's, and then one of Charles's colleagues. She saw a succession of sexual partners stretching as far as the eye could see. This, not guilt or shame, horrified her, this infinity of human connections, none of which would satisfy. At first she told Robbie everything. But in the winter of her junior year she grew silent, withdrawn, sulky. Robbie was too young, too vulnerable. She wanted to spare him her knowledge. But he pestered her. He wanted his sister back. And in the spring, as the ground thawed, so did Jo. She confided again.

"Robbie," she said, "it's time for a new approach. *I have decided we will squander our talents.* Toss them to the wind."

"But Jo," he said.

"We will amount to nothing in the eyes of our parents. We will swear a blood oath."

"But Jo..."

He didn't think he had any talents to squander, he wanted to say.

She took out a pocket knife, cut her thumb, then took his compliant hand and made a small cut in his.

"Ouch," he said, as she rubbed their thumbs together. Despite his reservations, he loved being close to Jo again; he reconsidered his mother's wisdom that problems can to some extent be understood. He thought about this until his brain ached. To make the pain go away, he finally accepted that he understood nothing.

~ ~ ~

"Of course they will stay here," Misha said the next afternoon, folding the laundered shirts with precision. "There's always room."

Twice a month the stars aligned to give Smith and Misha the same twenty-four hours free from work. Usually savored, today the day had taken on a vinegary taste.

"They'll stay at a hotel," said Smith, rolling socks into balls, army-style, side-arming them against the wall like baseballs.

"No, that's impossible. And rude. They are family and will sleep in our bed. We can sleep on the floor or," he paused, tilting his head as if to let one side communicate better with the other, "they can stay at Ivan's." Whenever Misha tilted his head in this fashion, his smile turned sly and Smith imagined a dialogue going on between the little Misha who'd lived his first eleven years in Kiev and the hip American Misha who had been constructed on top. It was like talking with two people.

"With Ivan! Mish, are you crazy too?" Two months after they'd met, after a night spent in the Bellevue Emergency Room, Misha had explained that Ivan was "a little bit bipolar." Two years later, Ivan's emotional life, its carnival ups and downs, was routine. To Smith, he was handle-with-care Ivan, but no longer a diagnosis.

"No, well, maybe not with Ivan."

"What's impossible is that they stay here. Have mercy on me, Mish. Please." Smith was tempted to spell out the letters to *mercy* and *please*. "They're my mother and sister, not just any family."

"Family is family. I don't understand your distinctions. Besides, there are obligations. No, I'm sorry. It's a no-brainer. They stay with us."

Misha's English was impeccable, but when he used idioms—"no-brainer," for example—there was an over-learned quality to it, a rumbling Slavic undercurrent. It was seductive and typically Smith succumbed. But Helena staying in his home would be unbearable. Eagle-eyed Helena was sure to spot the cracks in his hard-earned new life, her insights scalpel-sharp.

"They'll stay in a hotel." Smith upended the folded laundry and stomped into the bedroom, slamming the door behind him. He was embarrassed; Misha, a film school student at Columbia, would think the door slamming was out of a Bette Davis movie. But Russians were not above their own melodrama, he thought, in consolation.

The door opened a crack and Misha's head appeared. "I don't understand why we can't talk."

"There's nothing to talk about. You either get it or you don't."

"Get it? Get it? That you wish to treat your family as if they were strangers, or worse, like vermin."

Misha's cell phone chimed the opening chords to "Back in the USSR."

"Yes, Ivan. No. Yes. Yes. No. No. *Nyet.* Maybe, later." Smith's thoughts drifted to the rain forests again, the melting ice caps, the spread of diseases that had existed for eons in isolated jungles. These concerns frightened him but were easier to understand than family. This, Misha would never get. Feelings about family were like religion, Smith had learned since being with Mish. The differences were as profound as the approach to God defined by Catholics and Protestants, Jews and Muslims, Hindus and Buddhists. And just as irreconcilable. In Misha's world one was loyal to the death for family, even if they drove you crazy, even if they were crazy.

"Ivan says hello and that they can stay with him." He crawled into bed next to Smith and they lay side-by-side, facing each other, but not touching. Smith felt them breathe in tandem. Why was it so hard for Mish to understand? "Yes, your mother is a psychotherapist, and yes, she may be, as you insist, larger than life and so very demanding. But why," Misha had asked, "is this such a problem it cannot be solved? They are people. All people are too much of this, too little of that. What is the big deal, Smitty, if they love you?" Unspoken was Misha's loss, his mother's death in childbirth.

"In a hotel," Smith said.

"Okay, have it your way. In a hotel." He lifted Smith's chin up. "Smitty, look me in the eye?"

"I am."

"Yes, now, but lately only if I ask."

"Not true," Smith said, kissing him softly on each eye, feeling Misha stiffen, then tremble, brushing Misha's lips with his.

That night, Smith lay awake, eyes closed, while Misha slept, clinging to him lightly. Polar icebergs shone radiantly white under a full moon. They stirred, as if from a long sleep. His breath came in stops and starts, in synchronicity with the crack and groan of glaciers, shattering the Antarctic silence. The wind howled like a pack of wolves, like lunatics in an asylum.

~ ~ ~

The year before their divorce Charles and Helen had taken him to Los Angeles. A convergence of conventions for the parents. Jo had stayed behind. He'd been fascinated by the La Brea Tar Pits. He tried to grasp how the dinosaurs and countless other creatures could disappear from the earth. There was so much about life he did not understand. The black tar pit—its ability to trap and kill—was the unknown. It was infinite and lurking. That night he'd dreamed he was sinking in tar. He awoke before dawn: death, divorce, the end of what appeared solid, filled his mind. If the dinosaurs could be snuffed out, what chance did people have? He'd already sensed that Charles might leave Helen, that marriages, love, had endings. (Riding his bike around campus one day, he'd seen his dad holding hands with a young woman.) At the tar pits, it came to him that each ending was a rehearsal for death. He pushed back hard against this new thought. Still, it took possession of him.

Preoccupied, he kept to himself at school. But he was maturing, too. He'd become a strong swimmer and joined the swim team. He noticed the sleek bodies of other boys; they were children in September, whose muscles by April were sculpted as if each boy were a quick sketch by Michelangelo. One noticed his and suggested they fool around. The sex was quick and frequent. Robbie didn't care for Toby, but craved his touch. It puzzled him, this obsession with a boy he didn't like. He felt himself come alive only when he and Toby explored each other's bodies. Life in between was a matter of waiting, planning, dreaming of sex. He'd thought love should be a part of the equation, but it was not. There was no joy, just the pursuit of it.

He could not talk to Jo about it; it was his first real secret from her. During those thrilling, hurried minutes with Toby, he was ecstatic; he, Robbie Doddsworth, had a soul. A soul! In his boyish way he came to believe that the passion he felt with Toby was a sign that death was not the end, that there might be a God and a life after death, and that sex was the path to igniting his own pallid soul into being. Perhaps, he thought, wistfully, the dinosaurs hadn't known about sex.

~ ~ ~

Smith ambled home from work, savoring the late-night smells of East Seventh Street: of restaurant kitchens and garbage; the park, its dewy leaves and grass; the pungent aroma of weed; the air dense, sticky, oozing of sex and the instinctual. The streets were never empty, but after four o'clock there was a hush, a moment of stillness that could stretch to an hour, if you were alert to it. In this hush, Smith was wrapped in a cocoon, his thoughts clearer, less scrambled and edgy. He spat on his shirt to rub at borscht stains and lost himself in a fantasy: he'd come upon a man—strikingly ugly, but in a sexy, magnetic sort of way—lying in the street, dying from a stab wound. Smith would take him in his arms, cradle the stranger's head on his lap, raise the man's lips to his, breathing life into him as the cops swooped down and, confusing the borscht stains for blood, mistake the Pietà-like moment for an act of murder...

Damn! They would arrive tomorrow. Labor Day weekend ruined. No sleeping the day away. No beach. And why was Helena coming? He longed to see Jo. And then, again, he didn't. It had been almost a year. Jo had looked tired then; she'd settled into a routine at the travel agency and he'd heard of several men in her life, though she made them sound like such dweebs, so beneath her. Postcards from Paris, Venice, London—perks of her job—sounded like the self-possessed Jo of old. The last one breezily announced she was engaged to a dentist. A dentist! And a creeping *I know what's best for you* insinuated itself into her phone calls. Misha be damned. He was ambivalent. He had a new life, such as it was; Robbie Doddsworth was totally, thoroughly the past.

But Helena. She was so responsible with her patients. She never took vacations, not even in August. "Such a cliché," she'd say, year after year. In addition, there was her agoraphobia. A psychotherapist mom afraid of open spaces. By the time he'd left home for New York, she had improved from those grim days after the divorce; she could make her way around town—but two square miles was her limit. At two miles there was a cliff and a bottomless abyss, she explained. "Maybe you need new glasses," he'd said, not recognizing cruel until it was out of his mouth. And flying became unthinkable. Her agoraphobia, which had been so totally uncool when he still lived in Ann Arbor, had, up until now, proved a blessing since he'd moved to New York.

He found his favorite bench in the park, near the fenced-in dog walk. He was sweaty and tired, but still buzzed. The sky was a cloudy crystal ball, glowing gray from sleepy, half-lit buildings, street lights, and a moon near full.

He wasn't ready to see Helena yet. And maybe not even Jo. He was not finished, it occurred to him. He thought of hanging a sign around his neck: CAUTION. PERSON UNDER CONSTRUCTION. He laughed. Who else would find this funny? Misha might laugh, but he wouldn't really understand. Ivan would ask about it earnestly. Only Jo would get it. Smith believed that most people were complete, finished by his age, done deals as persons. He was the only one playing catch-up in life.

He needed more time.

And now the tears did flow.

Smith was on the cusp of leaving Misha. He'd been on this cusp for a long time. How long he could not pin down. He thought of it now—this cusp—as the line of stakes that make a picket fence: on one side comfort, routine; fenced-in, for better or worse, in sickness and in health, by Misha's at times exalting, at times unbearably deep commitment. On the other side: all he need do was run.

~ ~ ~

Misha's unqualified love had for a time been a wonder. He thought back to their first meeting. That he'd met Ivan first was a fact he often forgot. Walking in the park, he'd seen Ivan sitting on a bench. Smith was attracted to his dark good looks and regal posture, hard to place—exiled royalty, Smith imagined, from Spain or, perhaps, Persia?—and his incandescent smile, which shone on lonely, new-to-town Robbie Doddsworth. He thought it might be this very bench, which was why it was his favorite spot in New York. It had been Labor Day. He was anxious about starting at NYU; he didn't know anyone in New York. The sun peeked in and out from passing clouds. The stranger's smile came and went with the sun. Smith made the first move, so unlike his Michigan self, but it was the stranger who did the chatting, rat-a-tat-tat. When Smith suggested going somewhere for coffee, his voice going all soprano from nerves—a battle within between lust and shyness—Ivan patted him on the knee and said, "I'm waiting for my brother." Smith rose to leave but the stranger said with pride, "No. You'll like him. He's my twin."

So they waited. As the clouds grew thicker and the sun retreated, the stranger became quiet, which made Smith edgy. He'd not been in New York long enough. He didn't know the rules. He searched the sidewalk for another short, equally beautiful man with dark hair. Would he be just as chatty? Or indefinably different?

They waited and he glanced nervously this way and that. Up above, a flock of birds flew south; below, he studied pigeons and sparrows pecking at food and pebbles, candy wrappers and broken glass. Suddenly, the stranger stood. "Hi, bro," he said to a tall, fair-haired man with sad blue eyes and a big smile. The dark-haired man's face, which had grown still and remote, became animated, as if he'd been jolted alive by an electric current. The brothers gave each other a kiss to each cheek, which Smith recognized from foreign movies. They were older, he realized, easily twenty-three or -four, and he was tongue-tied shy. Should he slip away? He'd imagined ending up in bed with the brother of the radiant smile, but his taller twin—fraternal twins, it was now clear—had his own appeal. He had small ears like baby bats that stuck out at wide angles. The brothers switched between English and a wonderfully incomprehensible language. Smith felt his dull, Michigan self pale by comparison. The fair-haired brother gazed at him with those sad blue eyes. Then he smiled, a smile that seemed to strain his cheek muscles; it was a defiant smile, as if to say he was happy, could be happy, but happiness took work.

Smith had experienced lust, unrequited love, and a few inconsequential events that fell in between, but such longing as he felt now was new.

He wasn't sure if he was to end up with one of the brothers, both, or neither, but it was the man with the funny ears to whom he lost his heart, when, with a formal half-bow, he said, "My apologies. We have been rude, speaking Russian in front of such a handsome stranger." He offered a hand in greeting. It was large and warm, with long delicate fingers. "My name is Misha and presumably," he continued, extending his other hand out, palm up, as if presenting someone of great renown, "you've met my brother, Ivan?"

"Yeah," Ivan said, "I'm Ivan."

"Ivan the *Terrible* we sometimes call him."

"Ivan the *Terrific,* Mish," Ivan said, and both brothers laughed.

"My name is Sm-Sm-Smith," Smith stuttered, minting this new name on the spot.

"Hello, Mr. Smith," Misha said, earnestly.

"No, just Smith," he said, still holding tight to the stranger's hand. And with the new name, his New York self was born.

It was Labor Day, and they later declared it their anniversary, although it was a month before the stranger called. After they'd met, Smith had been all nerves, eventually giving up hope as the days passed, then near forgetting, with classes to take, books to buy; and Misha, finally, mumbling on the phone, all apologies—my father took ill, my brother's in California, please be my guest for dinner? I'd be so honored. The pasta was undercooked, the sauce too thin, too sweet, but, by then, who cared?

~ ~ ~

The agitated chatter of unseen birds announcing daybreak brought Smith back to the park and the present moment. He looked up toward East Eighth Street, toward home, where pink had softened the night sky's murky gray. Was leaving Misha the same as Chuck leaving Helena? A family dynamic? A repetition compulsion? He cringed at the language in his head. He had been trained by Helena to think this way. Helena would burrow in on the cause, the psychological trigger, while Chuck would shrug amiably, a disinterested nod to the infinity of cause and effect.

"Cusp," he knew from his dad, was a mathematical term, a curve crossing itself; and Smith saw his two possible lives—the one with Mish and the one without—reduced to mathematical curves snaking toward infinity.

I'm ill-equipped for this, he thought, facing up to the dread. I'm only twenty, after all. It was Louie's death that changed it all. But death and its aftermath could not be reduced to variables in an equation or the language of therapy. And it was a burden he carried alone: Mish and Ivan never talked about Louie in his presence. His name had become taboo. He'd tried, but Misha's face turned cold, his rosy cheeks paled.

The sound of garbage trucks laboring slowly up Avenue A silenced the noisy birds: these clumsy, monstrous trucks were the city's true announcers of dawn; birds were no longer necessary, he thought sadly, although he was relieved that there were still birds!

Smith bolted up. It was maddening. Damn Jo! She was supposed to protect him from Helena, not add to his burden. He kicked a can and returned to considering the rain forests. Smith kicked the can again, deciding that the indigenous peoples were, on balance, the victims in this drama, although the wormy bother of their selling out so cheap still gnawed at him.

Smith was not ready to face up to loss, not of the rain forests and the people who lived in them, not the death of people in general or particular. He sensed that he'd reached the beginning of an unexplored continent—honesty with himself—and in doing so, glimpsed, for the first time, Helena's courage. But he'd run aground on this: death's outline beneath Misha's pale skin.

The virus in his blood.

It was this he was poised to run from, not love.

~ ~ ~

Mother and sister stepped out of Ivan's cab in complementary pastel outfits: pale pinks, Helena; pale blues, Joanne. Each wore a straw hat: Helena's was large, oversized, suitable for the tropics; Jo's was smaller, more stylish. Each had a pastel ribbon that fluttered in the breeze.

The clothes irked Smith—their matching. Had Jo morphed into a clone of Helena? Perhaps planning a wedding did this to women.

Helena looked, in turn, at Smith, Misha, and Ivan. She blinked rapidly as if her eyes were taking snapshots. He had not seen her in two years. She was smaller than he'd remembered, prettier, younger looking, and more vulnerable. Her hair was cut short, almost boyish. But her dress, in the humid air, had lost any shape it might once have had. She was pale—odd for his mother, who worshipped the sun as much as she did the psyche. She looked bewildered. Helena had clung to her children after the divorce; she needed them like a vacuum cleaner needs dust, he'd once explained to Misha, who'd snapped, "She's your mother, Smitty." No need to say "Be grateful you have one."

"So?" she said. It was a gentle interrogatory *so*, spoken in Helena's velvety therapist voice. It was followed by a medium-strength hug that suggested meanings, and an earthy "Hi ya, sweetheart."

Smith sighed. She'd found her bearings. He was relieved, but also wary. "Hi, Helena," he said. "The hotel?"

"I thought we'd stop here first, sweetie, then freshen up later."

Jo lingered near the cab, standing by Ivan. Eyes downcast, she looked defeated, her dark, dramatic lipstick the only sign of her feisty self. Ivan gave her a small push toward Smith. She looked up at him, her eyes widening as if waking from a trance. Brother and sister embraced—too politely, he thought.

"Are you okay?" he whispered. She pulled away.

Misha, who had been standing to the side, abruptly stepped in and engulfed mother and sister in a long hug.

"Welcome," he said. "Please be very welcome." Misha was so courteous when he was nervous. Smith, usually touched, now found it irritating.

Helena took the hug as if it were an expected gift to a visiting potentate. Her look was now alert. He knew it well. Misha smiled too broadly. His eyes were unblinking.

"This is Mi-Mi…Misha," Smith said, unnerved.

"We have so much to talk about," Helena said to Smith in a stage whisper.

To Ivan, she asked, "Would you mind…?" pointing at the cab. Hadn't Jo explained who Ivan was?

"No problemo," said Ivan, his dark hair slicked-back and gleaming, his smile several notches too loud.

Ivan opened the trunk and emerged, balancing packages.

His mother and sister had come bearing gifts wrapped in paper of pale blues and pinks to match their outfits. Later, when unwrapped, the gifts were a large ceramic bowl; two books for Smith: from Jo, *Don Quixote,* and from Helena, *To the Lighthouse;* matching wool scarves, ski caps, and gloves for Smith and Misha; and a U of M T-shirt, sweatshirt, and tank top for Ivan. Also later, Smith would find an envelope in *Don Quixote* with a half-ounce of weed.

"So?" Helena asked again.

"What is it?"

"Are you all right? You don't look good." She touched his forehead. "Too thin," she muttered, as if attempting to recall lines from a play.

From Jo, impatiently: "Leave Robbie alone. You promised." But Helena, after glancing over at Misha, now turned her attention to Ivan, whose presence seemed to puzzle her.

"My brother," Misha said, still unblinking, pointing toward Ivan.

"Oh, yes. Of course."

Had she slipped from agoraphobia into Alzheimer's? Smith wondered.

"At your service, Mrs. Doddsworth," Ivan said, hand outstretched.

She took his hand limply. "I'm sorry, Igor. I'm, well, ...a little dehydrated."

Misha cringed, as if it were his mistake.

"Helena, it's Ivan, not Igor," Smith said, testily.

And Ivan: "It's okay, Smitty. Cut her some slack. Your mom's dehydrated."

Helena pulled out a pair of large sunglasses. She briefly examined Misha and Smith again, then craned her neck to take in the tenement building her son called home. A coat of industrial gray paint had been slapped over the original red brick, and the cornice and window ledges were purple. It stood as the one failure on East Eighth Street to attain the moneyed look of recent years.

She turned back to Smith, bringing a thumb to her lips, a gesture he recognized; a sign that she'd come to some sort of conclusion.

"We have so much to talk about," she said.

There'd been a time when he'd trusted her concern for him; that he'd loved her so much and still did, despite all this sidewalk awkwardness, took him by surprise.

"I'd kill for a Diet Coke," she said.

Misha's smile vanished.

"Diet Sprite, Pellegrino, wine, beer…" he said, now blinking furiously.

"That's fine," Helena said.

"Unacceptable!" Misha said. "I'll be back in a flash."

"A nanosecond, Mrs. D.," echoed Ivan.

Smith glanced at Joanne. She was the one who looked tired, thin. Her eyes dull. At least she'd not cut her long, luminous brown hair. "We will squander our talents," she'd said. They'd sworn to it. She'd stayed in Ann Arbor to work as a travel agent. The summer after high school he broke the news. He was going to college in New York. "New York," he said to Jo, "is a fine place to squander my talents." "Go for it," she'd said. And later, his discovery, as the plane gained speed, its nose lifting: what a rush it is to leave people behind!

With Misha off to buy Diet Cokes and Ivan, ignored, leaning against his cab, Smith stood alone with Jo and Helena.

"We can wait upstairs?" he said. It came out as a question, when he'd meant to sound strong, decisive.

"Okay," said Joanne. There was a vagueness in her voice that matched the way she looked: a shimmering mirage, a spring flower wilting in midsummer heat.

Helena looked again at the building and scrunched her nose. "I think it best we wait for your friend."

"Mom," said Joanne, stretching out the vowel.

The two women stared at each other. There seemed a standoff as to who would decide. Jo was sputtering into life. There was anger between them; it was old, familiar to Smith, but something about it was new. People change so quickly. It was so damn unfair!

He'd been away for a long time, he realized.

Then they both swiveled toward Smith. It came to him with a feeling of pride, like a balloon expanding in his chest, that he was their host—pride, which quickly dissipated into alarm.

"Let's... Let's... Let's..." he repeated, pausing between each word, waiting for a decision to emerge from his mouth, while the two women stared at him expectantly.

And then from Ivan: "He's coming! He's coming!" Jumping up and down, pointing, as excited as if a parade were arriving.

They all turned. Yes, there was Misha, who was walking toward them so fast that Smith feared he was going to stumble and fall face forward onto the pavement, but who reached them safely with his arms wrapped around two six-packs of Diet Cokes, just as a few drops of rain began to fall and the wind stirred, which had Helena and Jo reaching up to steady their hats.

Suddenly, Ivan shouted "Wait!" and dived into the cab. He emerged with two Fairway shopping bags. Offered up proudly. Another gift. Not from mother or sister, but Ivan's very own. Two bags. They all joined together in a shared curiosity, formed a circle and looked down into one bag, then the other.

"Apples, how lovely," said Helena.

"Apples, how nice," said Jo.

"Apples," said Smith, an uneasy observation.

From Misha, "Apples? So many?" with an angry stare at his brother.

And Ivan, eyes locked on Misha's, "Apples. What's your problem? The first of the season. From upstate. You know, fall, autumn, sweet and juicy."

As it was a gift—although unclear to whom—those assembled stood awkwardly, no one sure who should take the bags Ivan held out.

"Thanks, Ivan," said Smith, to break the tension. "We can always use apples."

And with those words they each stepped back, and the circle of curiosity that joined them was broken.

"Let us bring the gifts upstairs, right, Smitty?" Misha said. "We must show them our home."

"Yes, of course," said Helena. "That would be lovely."

They followed Misha up the stairs. At the first landing, Jo paused, took off her hat, and turned to Smith with an impatient tossing of her hair and several deep breaths of exasperation. Wordlessly she was confessing: "Why the hell did I ever agree to bring Mom?" and it meant the world to him.

~ ~ ~

The Circle Line Cruise around Manhattan. Ivan's idea. Smith thought it dopey, uncool, but once the boat left its dock Helena was mesmerized. "Robbie, can you believe I haven't been to New York since I was ten? Why did I wait so long?" she asked, tightening her grip on his hand. At last they were not in a confined space. What a relief! These past days had given Smith the chance to see Misha's need to be wrapped in an extended clan; Ivan, Louie, and Smith were the mold, but Misha had a larger vision in mind. Did Mish know this about himself? Smith had observed the way Misha clung to Helena as if she were his mother returned from the grave. Smith was equal parts touched, irritated, and spooked.

He pulled Joanne aside. "Let's take a stroll, Sis."

"Yes, please. You can be quite brilliant, little brother."

"So, a dentist?" he asked, smirking. They leaned against the boat's railing, far enough away from the others for privacy.

"Yeah, a dentist. You've a problem with that?"

"Yeah, I've a problem with that. It's called signing on for a boring life. A life sentence."

"It's called settling down, Robbie. It happens. It's called wanting kids. And besides, he's a cute dentist." She ran a hand through his hair, his enviable curls. "I'm glad you're growing your hair back. That skin-head look last year gave me the creeps."

"Don't change the subject."

"You picked that so-called subject, not me."

Caw-cawing seagulls swooped down from a clear blue sky. Brother and sister watched as two gulls fought over a fish that sparkled for a moment in the sunlight before both let go and it fell back into the river, kicking up a brief explosion of white foam.

"Whatever turns you on, Jo," he said. Not: You look so sad. And not: I'm losing you and I'm not ready. He put an arm around her shoulder and gave a clumsy squeeze. It was his job to save her; he owed her that.

"Robbie, you look like someone's died. Knock it off. I'm getting married like most people do."

"Most people aren't you," he said. The wind picked up and the pennants strung along the boat's many lines and cables snapped, sounding like a succession of slapped faces.

"He plays the piano, Robbie, jazz and classical. He reads poetry to me. He's great in bed. Does that satisfy you? It satisfies me."

"Oh, really? But he's still a dentist."

"He was born with cerebral palsy. He spent years in and out of hospitals. He walks with leg braces. He…"

"I'm sorry, Sis," Smith said.

"I don't want your apologies, Robbie, I want…" she paused and looked up at the empty blue sky.

"You have my blessings."

She caressed his cheek. "Yeah, you little idiot." Her eyes moistened. Were they tears?

"Don't cry, Sis." Finding the right words—and saying them—was new and strange to him. He felt powerful in a way that made him queasy; or was it the swaying of the boat?

"It's just the wind in my eyes."

"Yeah, right."

"I made up the part about cerebral palsy," Jo said, sheepishly.

"Fuck, why?"

"I don't know. Maybe to break through your thick skull." She gently tapped her knuckles on his forehead.

"Reading poetry's cool enough. So is playing the piano."

"But he can't do numbers to save his life."

"Even better."

They gave each other the Doddsworth family smile—a thin line of white teeth—a look that was ironic, amused, and maddeningly cryptic to outsiders.

"Here," she said, pulling a joint from behind her ear as if it were a magic trick.

"Cool, Sis." Two puffs and out tumbled: "Why's Mom here? Why the trip?"

"You tell me. She's turning sixty in December. I think it's the whiff of mortality people get at her age. And you are her only son."

"Give me a break."

"Well, you are. She needs me, but she misses you."

The boat's engine grumbled loudly as it labored against the gusting wind. Salt spray coated their faces. Waves smacked the boat's side harshly.

Smith leaned over the rail, a finger down his throat. "Ugh."

"Don't say you're any less dramatic than Mom, you dork," Jo said, adding a quick, hit-and-run kiss to his cheek. She stepped back and took a deep breath. "Are you okay, little brother?"

"I'm just fine, big sister. Okey-dokey."

"Really?"

"Yes, really." Smith had been waiting for her to ask about him and Misha. He wanted her to but he was ambivalent. He needed a booster shot, not meddling.

The wind calmed itself back into a breeze; the boat's engines resumed their soft, steady growl.

He gave her a goofy smile, his clown smile. She was supposed to tweak his nose, then he'd look at her in horror, hide his face in his hands and she'd pepper him with kisses until he'd laugh hysterically. It had been years since they'd played this game. But instead she stared at him, her eyes cool and gray.

"Can I ask one more itsy-bitsy question?"

"How itsy-bitsy?"

Her face was to the breeze, and fine strands of her long brown hair blew into her mouth. She pulled them away with a graceful, unconscious movement of her hand. He was fascinated. It was a gesture she must have mastered years ago, but he'd never noticed.

"Very, very itsy-bitsy."

Brother and sister huddled close. Smith glanced over his shoulder at Misha and Helena in an intense conversation, Ivan standing to the side, hands in pockets, smiling his smile, trying to find his rightful place when for now he had none. What were they going on about? He didn't trust Helena, her capacity for instant intimacy. He wanted to send a signal to Misha. Smith had once planned to study sign language. How wonderful it would be if he could send a silent warning Misha's way, encoded in a movement of hands and fingers, quick, delicate, precise.

"Kiddo, are you there? Don't go space cadet on me," Jo said, and squeezed his hand.

"I'm all ears."

Jo took several more deep breaths, as if courage were an inflated tire. "Are you careful?" she asked.

"Careful? Careful about what?"

"I don't know—looking both ways before you cross the street. Flossing after meals. You know, are you watching out for yourself?"

"Spit it out, Sis."

"You and Misha. Do you guys…take precautions?"

It was not like her to be evasive. She was nervous and now he understood why.

"You know?"

"Yeah."

"How?" he asked. Instead of anger he felt lighter, as if a long-lasting fever had abated.

"Does it matter?"

"No, not really, I guess. Okay, yes, it does matter."

"Ivan. Last year. Don't be angry with him. He meant well."

"He always means well," Smith said, relieved it had not been Misha. But what to say now? He and Misha were very safe, too safe; so safe that when he felt his greatest need for him Smith could, of late, barely tolerate his touch. That one time when they'd first met and Misha had told him he was HIV positive, they'd talked of it for hours, but never again. Back then he'd placed his bet on love over fear.

"You still haven't answered me. Are you guys playing safe?" He recoiled, stiffened. She let go of the railing, took his other hand in hers and grasped them both.

"Playing," he said. "*P-l-a-y-i-n-g*! It's not a freaking game, Sis." He'd talked to no one about his feelings because there were no words, or rather, to put them into words twisted them out of shape. And now, perhaps a little too stoned, he felt himself waist-deep in the black tar that had done in the dinosaurs: sinking, sinking, the tar rising to his throat, his mouth, pausing just below his eyes.

"Robbie…"

"Weren't we talking about Helena?" He pulled his hands free of hers and looked away. They—Jo and Helena—had come to mess with the new life he'd so carefully built. That was now clear. He felt closer to Misha, protective.

"That's the George Washington Bridge," he said, sternly, pointing up. "And that's Grant's Tomb," waving a hand vaguely at the Manhattan shoreline. "And there's New fucking Jersey."

"Calm down, Robbie. I trust you. Really."

"And that building there," he pointed wildly, "is, fuck, I forget what it is, Sis," and he took her into his arms as he'd never done before.

"Love you, too," she said.

Brother and sister held each other and rocked with the motion of the boat. When he opened his eyes he saw Ivan wave while walking toward them, rolling side to side, struggling to keep his balance. "What are you two talking about?" he shouted.

Smith whispered in Jo's ear, "We don't let Ivan do drugs. He's like, you know, fragile."

"I know," she said, softly, sadly. "What say we join the others?" She took his hand and they walked away as once they'd walked home from school, Ivan bouncing by their side.

"What say," he replied.

~ ~ ~

"Your mother's really cool," Ivan said. They were driving on the Brooklyn-Queens Expressway, returning from a visit to Louie's grave in

Staten Island. That Louie wasn't in his grave no longer seemed to matter. He'd been cremated but his old pal, Leo, had bought a grave site and a tombstone. "I need a place to sit and talk to him," he'd said.

The brothers went each month, but never together. For months Ivan had asked, but Misha begged off; then he'd go on his own the following week. A routine was established: Ivan the third Sunday of the month, Misha the fourth. Once, Smith asked if he could come along. "No," Misha had said. It was a slow, firm "no." It had the sound of a decision a lifetime in the making.

But Ivan liked company.

"Really?" Smith said. Helena and Jo were "doing" Bloomingdale's and Macy's, and Misha was at home, working. Smith wore a tank top and shorts; he was cold in the cab's air-conditioned chill.

"Yeah. But why do you call her Helena and not mother, or *ma mère*?" Ivan asked, the French a bit odd—it was not one of his languages—although odd and Ivan were sometimes hard to tell apart. One made allowances for Ivan. But tossing in a bit of French was new. Ivan had not been hospitalized in almost a year, not since Louie's death, although there were several near misses, and Smith and Misha were alert for the signs.

"No, why should I call her *ma mère*?" Smith asked, exaggerating the accent to needle him. Then he added gently, "Besides, her real name is Helen. Helen Smyth Doddsworth, Ph.D. Licensed to shrink heads and"—he paused to study Ivan's profile—"fearless at it."

"Don't get me wrong, Smitty, Helena's a beautiful name for a mother. Flowing, like silk, or a river."

"That's what she thought. 'Who could have imagined,' she said, 'how adding a letter, a simple, little, mind-its-own-business vowel, could transform a life?'" It had marked her rebirth after Chuck left. Smith had been dazzled by her then, her dark brown eyes enormous, dominating her face because of the weight she'd lost. Reborn, she'd seemed a cross between a princess and a wizard.

"That's very intriguing," Ivan said. "A real inventive lady." Ivan cooed a string of *ah's,* reminding Smith of whale song. He sighed. Whales and Ivan, both endangered species.

Smith envied Ivan, so pleased with this sound, this discovery. "You have the power to transform your life—it's within you," Helena would say to him and Joanne. It became the mantra for her workshops and TV appearances.

Ivan turned toward him, singing, smiling. "Eyes on the road," Smith said, when the cab wavered too close to an SUV. Envy turned into worry: was a fresh mania taking hold? It often began with infectious high spirits, but it always ended ugly. Smith recalled the sorrow in Misha's eyes the day he'd told him of Ivan's illness: "I'm telling you just so you should know." He'd cradled Misha's head in his lap, this man who was still a stranger.

"Don't worry, bro," Ivan said. He'd begun to call him "bro" of late, something which Smith both liked and was wary of. "Eyes are on the road, *but watch the hands,*" and Ivan lifted both hands and looked at Smith in a way that was—well, Smith didn't know what it was. It was canny, almost cunning, but it could be the beginning of crazy. It put Smith on edge, which he tried to hide.

"Ivan, um… Please…"

Ivan's hands returned to the wheel. "Had you going there. Admit it, Smitty."

Ivan patted him on the thigh and squeezed. Ivan, don't, he thought, please don't. It was a turn-on and it was scary. Very scary. Ivan was foreign, after all, affectionate, and very handsome, but also Misha's brother. Smith's mouth grew too dry for speech.

They rode in silence, broken occasionally by Ivan cooing those *ah's.* Smith stared out the window at passing cars and the blur of low-rise buildings in Brooklyn; across the East River, Lower Manhattan pushing its way into view like the bow of some kind of ship, a naval destroyer perhaps, willful and decisive; and up ahead, the Brooklyn Bridge.

How a simple letter can change your life. Helena had struck again. It was like sitting next to a demented but good-natured parrot. Smith ground his teeth. He began to sweat and bit at a fingernail, as Ivan's hand still rested on his thigh. If Ivan was going nuts, he'd timed it maliciously. Smith unrolled the window, gasping for air.

"You all right?" Ivan asked.

"Sure. Why?"

"No reason."

"Ivan, do you ever think about the rain forests? Do you worry about the ice caps melting?" Smith felt his voice rise and crack.

"Huh?"

"Ivan, do you know what's going to happen to Manila soon? To Bangladesh? Do you know what the glaciers are doing at this very moment? They're melting, breaking apart. Do you know that, Ivan? Do you worry about these things?"

The cab pulled up on East Eighth Street. A light rain began to fall.

"Why are you yelling at me?"

Smith gave him a quick hug and hurried out of the cab, then stuck his head back into the open window. "No reason," he said. "I was just wondering."

"Smitty?"

"Yeah, what?"

"Well... I wish I had a mother like yours."

"Really?"

"Yeah. You're a lucky guy." Then Ivan took off, tires squealing, leaving behind the sickly, sweet smell of burnt rubber.

The rain became steady. From far off he heard the faint rumble of thunder. But Smith was still as a statue. He willed himself to move, to take out his keys, unlock the door and walk up the stairs, but he was stuck. This wasn't how *lucky* should feel. In his wallet, creased from countless foldings and unfoldings was the ticket to Antarctica, the date tomorrow; *how something so simple can change your life,* he thought. No one knew. What a rush it would be to leave all this behind. He'd be able to think clearly again. Endings, he understood; he could choose the kind. Leaving is what I do best, he thought, unsure if this was his own insight or Helena's voice in his head.

And was he leaving Misha or that virus? He was ashamed. He felt pathetic. Would it make any difference to Misha? Who could he talk to? Once, when Louie was alive, he'd teased Smith during a walk around the park. "A *constitution,*" Louie called it however often Smith said "It's a *constitutional,* Louie." Smith now laughed and wiped away a tear. "Ask me for advice," Louie had said. "You never do. I'm an old man. That's what we're good for."

"Okay, how about your best shot of wisdom."

"Wisdom isn't vodka, Smitty. Give me a situation. Set the scene, as my Mishka would say."

"I don't know. Can't think of one."

"Smitty, there was a war in my country like I hope you never see. There's not much to learn from war except it stinks. But there was this time once, I wasn't much older than you, when artillery shells were falling all around. I couldn't think, let alone move. I shit in my pants, if that makes it any clearer. And this officer, a major, who'd been around, you could see from the scars on his face… He grabs me and says, 'Boychik, we can't stay here, so I'm going to say this once: if you find yourself in hell, keep walking.'"

"That it?" Smith said, confused, but wondering if Louie had known he was terrified and was giving permission, maybe sizing Smith up as too puny for the job of taking care of his son.

"Yes. Now let's play a game of chess in which, as you Americans say, 'I will wax the floor with you.'"

"It's *mop,* Louie, not *wax.*" He'd almost called him Dad.

"Same difference."

Smith was now soaked. He stood no more than twenty feet from the park where he and Louie had talked. A loud clap of thunder startled him. No, it was not the time for leaving, not today, not tomorrow, not yet.

~ ~ ~

Smith was early. Four coffees at home. Nerves ragged. He ordered a pot of tea and waited. He'd been surprised when Helena named a Chinese restaurant on Third Avenue. "We need to talk alone, us two," she'd whispered, slipping him a note last night; it had the name and address of a place he'd never heard of. The note, the whispers—it felt clandestine, as if they were spies. He didn't like that she knew of places in New York.

"We need time together without your little Misha," she'd said.

He poured tea into a small ceramic cup. It was decided: he'd not put up with her games! But she had a way of making him feel important, the lead actor in her psychodramas. It was such a cliché. He was such a cliché: the gay boy with a special relationship with his mother. He groaned inwardly and pulled his baseball cap down. If she can't see my eyes, I'll have an edge.

He gazed out the restaurant's large window at a handsome black man leaning against a car, holding a skateboard by his side. The silver wheels glittered in the sun. A slow grin spread on the man's face…an *I dare you* grin. The man with the mocking, lazy smile winked at him. It was a turn-on, for sure. Still, it would be another cliché: the black man and the skinny white boy from Michigan.

He felt blood rush to his groin, and the sensation of tiny pinpricks on his palms, his cheeks. He struggled to breathe; it was desire and he was tempted.

"Hi, hon," Helena said, floating into the seat across from him. She dropped a Bloomie's bag on an empty chair and leaned over to plant a kiss just to the side of his mouth. She was dressed in khaki shorts and a white U of M T-shirt; around her neck was a long blue silk scarf.

"Hi," he said.

"So," she replied, "alone at last," rubbing her hands playfully. She looked at the dark circles under her son's eyes, his unshaven cheeks, the napkin he was nervously picking apart.

The black man gave him an exaggerated shrug and took off.

"Yeah, obviously," he said.

"You're looking pale, sweetie." She fingered her scarf.

"The ozone layer, you know. Can't be too careful these days."

"Very funny."

A waiter took her arrival as his cue to appear.

"Order something, Mom." Calling her *Mom;* he'd give her that today.

"I'll have one of those," she said, "and that one, over there," pointing at various men on the street.

He laughed. "Where's Jo?"

"She's out with your little Misha and his very handsome brother."

"Misha's not little. Please stop calling him that."

"Let's not fight, sweetie. Okay?"

She tugged on his fingers as she had done when he had been very young and upset. He clenched his teeth to hold back a smile.

"Please, sweetie. Let's have a nice afternoon. It's been two years."

"Okay, okay." He held her hand in his and gave that smile. She'd come a long way, he had to concede. After the divorce, she'd retreated to her room, eaten almost nothing, and grown unnaturally quiet. She lost twenty pounds. It came to him and Jo that she was starving herself to death. They'd taken turns spoon-feeding her baby food. Over many weeks, they'd coaxed her out of the house. He was shaken again by the memory of his mother trembling during the short walk to the car, son holding one arm, daughter the other. Agoraphobia on top of anorexia. He'd loved her then more than ever before.

The waiter hovered over them. "I think you should order, Mom."

"Hmmm… I'll have…whatever it is they're eating," and she pointed to the next table.

"I'll have the same," he said, not hungry, not caring.

Smith poured them each some tea.

"Thanks, Robbie."

"Smith," he said, tersely.

"Okay, sweetie… I mean, thank you, Smith." They both laughed.

She looked to him like just another person in New York and he wondered if they could have a normal relationship, might even be friends. A new idea. This was going forward, not backwards.

The waiter returned, deftly arranging steaming plates and bowls on their small table.

Helena surveyed the food, picked up her chopsticks, hesitated, and then asked, chopsticks pointing at Smith, "So, how are things going with Misha?" Her voice was smooth, noncommittal, a therapist in full-interview mode. "Are you two happy together?"

"Happy enough. Plenty happy." He tensed, certain he knew where this was leading. But instead, a winsome smile and an "I'm glad for you both" led to an easy silence between them as they sipped their hot and sour soup and ate their Szechwan beef and eggplant, listening to the rattle of the air conditioner and the murmuring of lunchtime voices. Yes, perhaps they could be friends.

"Hon," she said, tentatively. He noticed a piece of food, something green, stuck to her front teeth and fought not to giggle. It looked deliberate, as if she were a clown and the tooth, makeup. "Honey, there's this spot." He thought she meant the food stuck to her teeth and was about to say in their newfound friendship, I know. "The doctor's found a spot. On a breast."

Smith flinched. "Oh," he said. He almost added, "Whose breast?" but stopped himself: he was emptied of feeling; then a wordless terror filled the void.

"Robbie…" she began. She looked at his face, which had gone pale, almost gray. She reached out and touched his unshaven cheek.

Smith looked past her at a man across the room. His hair was a white mane, his face creased, rough, pitted, as if he'd once been scalded with boiling water. When he caught Smith looking at him, he mouthed some words that Smith couldn't make out but that seemed to be a taunt of some kind. Then he threw back his head and laughed; Smith quickly looked away, back into his mother's expectant eyes.

"Oh," he said, again. "How serious?" His voice level, calm. There was that familiar pull again, to sit by her bedside, to hold her hand. But what about Misha? Didn't Misha need him too? Misha had Ivan. Was Ivan enough? Would Misha's life crumble if Smith left him? Smith had never considered this possibility that Misha depended on him. Being a man, Smith concluded, meant taking a stand…one family or the other!…or was it every man for himself?

"They don't know yet," Helena said. "I'll take more tests when I get home." She reknotted her scarf. Smith looked around, expecting stares, but there were none. The waiters navigated soundlessly between tables. He looked for the man with the long white hair and horrid face, but he was gone. This was what he loved about New York: a mother close to tears, her terrified son—*a scene*—and no one notices, or if they do they'll be damned if they let it show.

"I'm sorry, Mom." He tried to make the words sound as if they were from one friend to another; but a friend would be stunned, compassionate. If he had a soul, a *dusha,* he'd know what to say. He imagined that he could disappear, that he could stand aside and watch this scene between mother and son, study it, learn from it, anything but be a part of it.

"Robbie, you won't have me around forever. You do know that."

"I know," he said, pulling the baseball cap down over his eyes.

~ ~ ~

That night, Smith was startled awake. He was trembling. Sweat-soaked. He'd been frightened by a dream he couldn't recall. He slipped out of bed and walked to Misha's side. Misha slept facing the window, his breath even and steady. Moonlight left him half in darkness, half luminous. He snorted, then turned away, kicking at the sheet that had covered him, all of him now in shadow. Smith studied his spine, his neck, the muscles of his back, and his hair, unruly in sleep.

He tiptoed naked into the living room. He could see the moon through the barred window. It was a yellow summer moon, a slice nicked off short of full. He felt as if he had entered a stranger's house.

On the kitchen table was the ceramic bowl, Jo and Helena's gift, filled with Ivan's apples. It had a glazed pattern of thorny fantastical flowers. He wondered if it was from an elegant boutique or a Target, bought at the last minute.

He sat down. The trembling grew worse. What had the person who'd painted the bowl intended? Were the flowers a vision or was there no intent at all?

Smith was scared and he was angry. He took one apple, bit into it, spat it out, and threw the apple across the room. Then another and another. Soon the floor was covered with apples, each marked by a single bite.

He crawled under the table, brought his knees to his chest and held them tight. He lost track of time. Then, mysteriously, Misha was touching him on the knee and the room was filled with daylight.

"Smitty," he said. "Are you all right?" Again and again, "Smitty, Smitty, Smitty…" Misha kneeled down and their faces were inches apart. "Robbie?" he asked and Smith looked up. On Misha's face, that defiant smile. He wore his enormous white bathrobe. Smith had laughed when he'd first seen Misha swallowed by it. Misha nervously brushed away hair that fell over worried eyes that had never looked so intensely blue.

"I don't know why, but I can't anymore," Smith said, and began to rock.

"What do you mean?" Misha sounded like there was a damp cloth covering his mouth, as if the room was filled with smoke and breathing was dangerous. "Please come out from there. Please."

Smith asked himself: What do I mean? But there was no reply. He remembered a therapist with a pipe asking him, "What's your first memory? Your very first?"

"Cold water," he'd said. Some kids had pushed him into a pond. Jo had walked him home, holding his hand.

"Please come out," Misha said and pulled harder on his arm. Smith gave in. They stood, and then Misha opened his robe and wrapped the two of them inside. It was warm and Smith stopped trembling.

It was a mistake to have let Helena and Joanne come. And it was a mistake, this new family; it was a mistake to have stayed.

"I don't know what I want," he mumbled.

"Does anyone?" Misha said and held him close.

"*Kakoi koshmar!*" he whispered into Misha's ear.

"Yes, indeed, what a nightmare! Who taught you to say that?"

"Louie."

"Papa?" Misha held Smith's face in his hands, a challenging look, as if Smith were a medium invoking Louie's spirit.

What he'd meant to say was "I love you" in Russian.

It was Labor Day, their anniversary, but that other phrase, spoken by Louie last year on Thanksgiving, had wedged itself in memory.

"I'll make some coffee," Misha said. He gave Smith his robe and sat him down in a chair.

Smith watched Misha put a filter into the coffeemaker, measuring the grounds, adding water precisely. He was so very familiar. He opened a cabinet, took out two mugs, placing them on the table. Only then did Misha bend to pick up the apples, not asking about them at all, as if, yes, he did this every morning and would all the mornings of his life.

About the Editor

Peter Dubé is a Montreal-based writer and the author of the novel *Hovering World, At the Bottom of the Sky,* a collection of linked short stories, and most recently *Subtle Bodies,* a fictional—and fantastical—biography of surrealist René Crevel set on the day of his suicide that was a finalist for a Shirley Jackson Award. He is also the editor of the anthology *Madder Love: Queer Men and the Precincts of Surrealism*. In addition to his fiction, Dubé is a widely published cultural critic with articles having appeared in journals such as *Canadian Art, Spirale* and *ESSE*. In this capacity he is also a contributing editor for *Ashé Journal* and a member of the editorial board of the visual arts magazine *Espace Sculpture*. You can visit him online at peterdube.com.

PETER DUBÉ

www.ingramcontent.com/pod-product-compliance
Lightning Source LLC
Chambersburg PA
CBHW030412310726
48979CB00002B/385

* 9 7 8 1 5 9 0 2 1 2 2 6 4 *